T0354500

The Birthmark

Bernard Wendelin

BALBOA.PRESS

A DIVISION OF HAY HOUSE

Balboa Press books may be ordered through booksellers or by contacting:

Balboa Press
A Division of Hay House
1663 Liberty Drive
Bloomington, IN 47403
www.balboapress.com.au
1 (877) 407-4847

Because of the dynamic nature of the Internet, any web addresses or links contained in this book may have changed since publication and may no longer be valid. The views expressed in this work are solely those of the author and do not necessarily reflect the views of the publisher, and the publisher hereby disclaims any responsibility for them.

The author of this book does not dispense medical advice or prescribe the use of any technique as a form of treatment for physical, emotional, or medical problems without the advice of a physician, either directly or indirectly. The intent of the author is only to offer information of a general nature to help you in your quest for emotional and spiritual well-being. In the event you use any of the information in this book for yourself, which is your constitutional right, the author and the publisher assume no responsibility for your actions.

Print information available on the last page.

ISBN: 978-1-5043-2008-5 (sc)
ISBN: 978-1-5043-2009-2 (e)

Balboa Press rev. date: 12/09/2019

Chapter 1

D r Syd James came to the top of the back flight of stairs, opened the door panting as he entered the Coast Hospital's Labour ward. The two middle aged Midwives smiled and relief flowed as he acknowledged them. Busy night so far. Mrs Jing Dang was well advanced and ready to make her baby arrive. Syd James scrubbed up while he had a chance.

"Sarah, what point are we at please?"

"She's dilated 8-10cm and waiting for your assistance and the baby to move into position. Said it's not going to happen without you. Puts us old girls out of work."

Syd smiled, loved Sarah's dry sense of humour. He moved quickly and joined the Mum to be.

"All right Jing, let's get it on. Hi Mr, Dang –nice to meet you at last."

A clearly agitated Chinese gentleman shook hands as he sat holding his wife's other hand. Jing swore at Loui her husband in their dialect. Translation would be difficult but 'you bastard' in English might cover it. Mr Dang said nothing but beads of sweat were forming on his forehead and nose. In ten minutes, smiles and encouragement accompanied their baby boy delivered in a rush with no problems.

Little bleeding –perhaps 40-50mls from Mrs Jing. That equals a very good result. Sarah took the baby to weigh and clean up in the room adjacent to the birthing suite. Sarah noticed the birth marked eyelids immediately but did her duty and presented a clean, wrapped up little person to Mum. There would be notes in the paperwork later with the evaluation of the newborn infant.

Another name for strawberry birthmark is haemangioma of infancy, simply they are red raised and lumpy areas. In this case, newly arrived Simon Dang had both eyelids only, affected remarkably. It was a trivial disfigurement and with eyes open it was not confronting, but a new baby's eyes are closed. Red sunglasses seemed apparent on the child. Simon's mother blamed herself and questioned her memory of the pregnancy for unsatisfied wishes. Her culture pointed to that. In the balance, she knew that any birthmark near or on the eye will bring wealth. Her baby boy had two. Jing hoped for a life path for Simon reflective of wealth. There are all sorts of folklore and superstition about birthmarks and what they mean. This includes strawberry birthmark which can stop growing and gradually disappear in the child's early years.

As time went on Simon's distinctive eyelids remained through adolescence. Simon could enter a room and know which people present he should keep away from, he felt a presence of danger without concentration, and it came naturally. At age seven, Simon heard things at night whilst in bed. Simon mentioned it to his Father in passing over breakfast. Simon's mother stopped her washing up when she heard the statement. Jing came and sat with Simon, an arm over his shoulders as his Father across the table explained it proved to be the spirits of those long dead in the house mopping floors and moving about the kitchen. In other words–going about their business. Simon's Dad, Loui, also heard these noises. Simon's mother had slept on. Loui Dang became a confidant to his only son from that moment.

Years later Simon heard his parents discussing the backyard and how it sloped slightly the wrong way. They both wished for a flat backyard such as it was. Simon went out that night and laid on the lawn for an hour. In the next week shrubs from seed took hold of the lower border evening up the lawn. It now looked like a lawn bowls or Croquet green. Much to Simon's parents delight, they never realised. How could anyone explain? Simon kept it all to himself.

Simon Dang blossomed into an excellent student and negotiated high school by avoiding all sports activity. He preferred to read and was a first class nerd. He was bored with the curriculum and fantasised his way forward on many days by keeping quiet and listening to the rhythm of his thoughts which kept putting mathematical type problems to the forefront. The Maths text set he had already mastered and the teachers left him to it as Simon was gifted and talented in academic pursuits. Simon was no troublemaker.

Simon was also adept at palmistry. He had no pre-conceived ideas with this skill of his own but could read and analyse a palm with accuracy. Simon regarded it as a party trick.

In some cases, he didn't need to look at the palms to 'read' subjects. When Simon got older he realised that he could make money from this uncommon skill as many people were prepared to pay with cash for this kind of information.

People were fascinated by Simon's appearance, even though the port wine birthmark stain had paled to a red tinge as he got older. He was easy going, a nice bloke who had skills that were irregular. As a good Mathematician/actuary Simon found employment in an Insurance company. Life was coming together for his prospects and he had a boost in the second year of his career. Simon had several episodes of correcting predictive values in the superannuation arm of the company. His colleagues were unimpressed at first when the figures were presented. Time proved the work a milestone and spot-on accurate. This work gained the attention of his bosses and they moved him up to the Executive area as an Advisor on many projects where business matters and predictive values intersected. Simon ran through many of the decisions like a hot knife through butter. The CEO and Business development staff were astounded. Simon's hit rate was 98%. Simon as an advisor was an asset, consequently he became a very busy young man.

Chapter 2

At age 24, the Government Insurance watchdog staff attended a Financial Conference where Simon gave a presentation on his favoured predictive values in Insurance. They were impressed by Simon's presentation content and his manner as the wiz kid from Insurance Australia Corp. Simon fielded audience questions post presentation with aplomb, he was applauded and there was plentiful discussion.

The Government recruiters were informed and travelled from Canberra, to attend an arranged a lunch in Sydney to talk to Simon about his future. Simon at first thought it was just the networking that goes on at Conferences so agreed to a meeting only to finalise their enquiries. Simon did not want to work for the Government, sure that the Government had plenty of staff who could match his financial skills. Simon had no ambition to work in the public service but investigations into Simon's background and history went ahead and were thorough. When they at last decided to discuss Simon's future there was a delay. Simon was on annual leave surfing, beating many to the punch each day for waves on his board. He could read the wave pattern better than many and maybe predict the next set of rideable waves. It reduced his fatigue paddling back and forth. Simon thrived on a few hours sitting on a board 80 metres off the beach in sparkling conditions. Little wind and a three metre swell always saw a crowded break with the sun beaming down on a cloudless early morning. Time spent in the ocean was the best. And therapy. Clean environment, exercise and some f...ing great friendships arrived from surfing. Surfers love to swear!

The meeting with the Government guys was at first very uncomplicated. Simon reserved judgement as the recruiters he encountered were strong and serious but good blokes. Simon could tell, their presence was mild and welcoming. Simon saw their furtive glances at his eyes, not uncommon. He explained his 'condition', tongue in cheek;

"It depicts death or wounds from a previous life. Or perhaps your birthmark on your ear enables you to be a good listener. I should mention a birthmark on the palm of your hand which is covered by your fingers clenched equals money in the bank!"

Simon threw in some wild speculation to test their mettle and sense of humour.

"People who have no birthmarks died of natural causes in their previous life."

The taller official named Norm thought all that was hilarious bullshit and responded.

"I accept your worthless explanation for what it is. Simon, you hide your extraordinary abilities to protect yourself. I understand. I would like to turn the discussion that way. Could you answer some other questions? It is a quiz but please stick to facts as you see it and develop your answer for us if you can."

Simon sat non-plussed as he could usually get himself out of these situations without explanation. These guys were not buying it. Simon paused and thought this free lunch was proving tricky. He tried to be cool and honest, they had the credentials and he did not feel like a victim.

"Simon, you have solid smarts we could use. The applied mathematics in your talk was superb. Our view of your Insurance 'predictive values' talk was in a word 'impressive'. Without performing many investigations, we found evidence of the extraordinary associated with you in the recent past. Are you able to explain your enhanced predictive value analysis work to non-mathematicians like us? Please remember we are not spies!"

"No. Not so you would accept it. Basically, I have succeeded in quantifying choice. I can offer an example, a man faced with a choice of a new car versus a second-hand utility –there is no choice factor. Sorry, there are a very small minority who would choose the utility. But as risk calculations and analysis goes the <u>choice</u> in timing of retirement or purchase/investment has been identified in more detail."

"Then.....?"

The Government recruiters, Norm and Walter looked at each other.

"Gentlemen, I am a believer in God. I was born with haemangioma of the eyelids, my parents and everyone usually treated me well. I do not feel like a freak, the skills you talk about are an extension of business and applied mathematics. I have been able to add a little to current knowledge. That's about it. I cannot predict the future in our wonderful country where a bloke can determine his own future –correct?"

The questioners from the Government were not prepared for this line of argument. Walter, however, produced a list of reported extraordinary events and work outcomes involving Simon.

"Simon, I believe what you believe about yourself. We have an investigative list which I hope to discuss? Should I commence reading from my list?"

"Guys I am an unimportant slave to an Insurance company. What do you really want?"

"We are here to establish a link, and evaluate you as a candidate for our staff. Our task, as humble recruiters for our Government is to identify people with talents that fit our criteria. Simon that's you, humble as you are. We offer a gateway to very few individuals."

"Do you want evidence from me? It's like asking a magician how it's done."

"No. We have a proposal and wanted to meet you. The detail can wait Simon, you are a person of interest.

I personally would like to hear what it is that you want?"

"Acceptable question at last. Forgive my passion, but I want a clean ocean and environment. I want Politicians with some ticker! I want a fair shake treaty for the Indigenous First people of this country. We already have a great nation and a fair go. Let's fix the Climate changes and eliminate the self-importance of the deadshits in Canberra. That should be enough for you."

Norm and Walter felt they were beaten as there was nothing they could offer after that. Norm challenged Simon.

"Could you read my palm by the way?"

"In the blink of a birth marked eye."

Simon waved at Norm to put out his right hand out and looked carefully. Both Government guys looked on with concentration and interest.

"Let's see. A single man with some dark and stormy nights, sir. Your life line is strong but your heart line reveals some trouble. There is purity in your soul and an energy to defy the odds. Back the grey horse on Saturday at Randwick, race five. That will be $20."

Simon winked and smiled. To him it was entertainment.

"Am I correct? Norm are you single?"

Norm nodded, the Government guy did not look content, if anything he looked crestfallen. Walter laughed at his colleague's discomfort. After a brief pause, Norm and Walter paid for lunch, shook hands and presented Simon with their business cards. Simon knew this lunch had resolved nothing and they would be in contact again.

"Before you go, you should know one thing. I am nocturnal and work from home. An arrangement I will not change. Money will not sway my decision to any proposal. Thank you, gentlemen, for lunch. I enjoyed your company-thanks."

Simon, next day, pursued his routine and forgot about the lunch. He received a letter from Canberra a fortnight later by registered post. It contained an invitation to Canberra to meet the Department Head.

Simon summoned the courage to talk to his CEO weeks later. His boss held Simon's letter and sucked in his cheeks at the proposal.

"Simon, these windy bastards want you in Canberra, how do you see it?"

"Not interested. I like the beach and Canberra is full of bureaucratic so and so's as you know."

His boss's eyes were drawn to the eyelids as Simon sat without being asked. Simon did not enjoy being pressured. As an environmentalist and a lover of the ocean, the Government's performance and policy was a red rag to the bull. Last thing he wanted was to work for them. Simon composed a letter in reply.

A year later, Simon, still with Insurance Australia, read a report from the Bureau of Meteorology tracking tropical cyclone Ferdinand in North Queensland. The Insurance Company stood to pay out hundreds of millions if widespread damage occurred in a major centre like Mackay in far north Queensland's coast.

Simon reviewed the forecast positions and checked the probable area bounded by latitude and longitude readings. The Bureau's probability of the 'probable track area' was 70% accurate according to their predictions. Short term erratic departure of the tropical cyclone from the general direction of movement may occur. Simon checked the infa-red satellite image and calculated the time difference of the reception of the image and the position of the cyclone. He rechecked his predictions and realised something was amiss. Simon called through to the Bureau and identified himself as the Insurance Analyst and was switched to the Bureau's tracking Team Leader, a Mr John Burke. Their discussion was lengthy about Simon's calculations and the variations in the size of the 'potential track area' corresponding to the forecast hours. The Bureau published error statistics of the forecasts issued in past years. The Team Leader had listened to Simon and knew the uncertainties in locating the centre of the tropical cyclone. Simon waited patiently for feedback. The interval was two cups of tea before Simon picked up his phone.

"John Burke here Simon. We re-calculated and find it all correct, but you have estimated the path in a non-standard manner. Your factor of uncertainty is not used by this team. We stick with our forecast. Oh, by the way, we agree on the timing to pass over the coast. If your calculations prove more accurate by the hour as per your chart, we shall talk again. Thanks, and all the best to you."

Simon submitted his calculations, predictions and an accurate account of the conversation for his boss as a matter of record. Job done. 48hrs is a long time to wait for winds of 200kms+, but the people on the coast of North Queensland prepared as only they can.

The tropical cyclone tracking by the Bureau proved Simon correct with his probability table hitting 90% accuracy. Government officials were on the scene in the aftermath of the bad weather with large scale losses to property and stock. $50 million in estimates. A week later Norm and Walter organised a meeting at the head office of Insurance Australia with the CEO, Ron Beardsley and Simon Dang.

"Mr. Beardsley, your man, Simon Dang, has outpointed the Bureau of Meteorology predictions. The costs must be confirmed but the percentage improvement from this one tropical cyclone could be substantial. Simon Dang has brought us here today. We seek your co-operation."

Ron Beardsley nodded and said;

"Our Company has been onsite settling claims from day one of this mess. I agree that a proportion of the damage could have been avoided, but Gentleman tropical cyclones are unpredictable. A factor we put in all our calculations."

Norm and Walter agreed, and in unison looked at each other. It was looking like an Abbot and Costello routine with them. Simon remained silent.

"Our Government requests the services of Simon Dang in co-operation with the Bureau of Meteorology. This new factor must be considered in improving outcomes."

Simon enquired.

"How will this work? I intend to co-operate if you support me."

"That detail commences with a training mission and the assistance we will give in the publication of Simon's data and method. The rest of the Scientific community will want to utilise the information."

"OK with me. I need time to formulate a publication?"

Simon replied, then looked at Ron, the CEO.

"Your routine work we can offload to another Actuary. OK gentlemen?"

"Done. Thank you both."

The Government pair departed.

"Ron, thanks to you I am working as a weatherman, can I have a Consultant with a short black skirt?"

Ron Beardsley laughed and pointed to the exit.

Simon got home and thought. It was not a prediction....... 'I have just made my first and last mistake.'

Chapter 3

Days went by and Simon felt eyes on his neck, noticed people watching him, surveillance even grocery shopping. Anonymity for Simon is the thing that evaporated, giving access to the Government to his time and eventually all the secrets of my life. Simon had to accept it.

Simon was given unprecedented clearance in the Government IT systems. They already knew all about him. Surveillance of his life and activities returned to normal scrutiny. The list of tasks directed his way was varied, some he could immediately assist.

Stunned Public servants would receive a call directly to embrace the issue and then a fax would arrive in a short time with directive action. They could act immediately on Simon's advice. Each Government department that had tasks assigned to Simon benefitted in some way. A pro-active Government delighted not only the bosses. The NSW Police got in the queue. They sought a serial killer currently responsible for a mounting body count, Detectives were keen to enlist the help of the 'The Birthmark.'

NSW Police strategy to combine resources to track down a faceless murderer was based on desperation and necessity, this killer targeted rich young women from Sydney's Eastern suburbs, and he (or she) was clever. They contacted Simon via the Federal Police Investigative Unit. The tension from NSW Police was high, they needed a breakthrough.

Averil Dunning stood alone at the bus stop waiting to get home. A distorted voice was heard behind her. She ignored it, looking at her phone, no surprise there. Averil was in her training gear after Netball training, catching up with phone messages. The voice continued.

"You don't know me and please don't be frightened."

Averil's phone rang as she turned towards the voice, then instinctively pressed the button to stop the call.

"What is it?"

The unseen voice said;

"I feel absolutely ill. Could you use your phone and call an ambulance? Thanks."

The voice trailed away and Averil quickly called 000 but then pocketed the phone as she then heard a falling person behind the bus stop in the darkness. Averil went to assist. Too late to protect herself, Averil was silenced forever around the throat by an unseen but very strong female. The smell of Body lotion was Averil's last recollection.

Commuters found her body next morning after Police were alerted by Averil's Rose Bay parents. The news services had a field day and apprehension swamped the Eastern suburbs. This was number 3. Police activity went up substantially and behind the scenes, supplement Detective manpower was transferred to solve these murders. Public scrutiny of Police news and interest in the murders went through the roof.

Simon Dang was formally briefed on these murders by his local Maroubra Police. They offered all resources and co-operation. Simon now felt the pressure he detested. Time to remain calm and hop to it. He reasoned as he poured over the available information as a very motivated man. Simon, found he now wanted this person hunted down. Simon's perennial interest was predictive value, or in this case predictive behaviour. Simon asked himself.

'Why murder innocent young women?'

Simon's major dilemma was that crime was out of his league and kicking himself for accepting the plea for assistance. He disciplined himself to do the things required. So Simon reviewed all the murders, then he went surfing at Bondi. He needed to contemplate on a few intangibles. Simon got home to find his now best friends, the Police on the veranda doorstep. They introduced themselves as Jim and Paul.

"Come in gentlemen. Give me a moment."

Simon stowed his surfboard and towelled down. He made the two Officers tea. They sat patiently. Both ofthem silently wondering if they were wasting their time with Simon Dang.

"OK. What news can you share?"

"To summarise, Mr Dang there is a developing theory that this is a woman who can get close to the victims, gain their confidence and cause these events."

A pause as the Detective looked at his notes. Simon liked this Policeman who was at great pains to be correct.

"Also, we are wary, as all so far have been public places. All have been strangulation with no prints. A suspect who is female, strong and with an unremarkable accent. Age and description-sorry, we are whistling into the wind. Why murder young women in public would be a good question?"

Simon drank some tea. He looked steadily at the Officers to offer his genuine support.

"Gentlemen. I sympathise and want to assist. Best help I can give is a request for a piece of clothing, something the perpetrator wears. A personal item-for me I can link it, I hope. Sounds bizarre perhaps but identity in this case can be confirmed that way. This person will make an error in judgement, just as we all do. Hopefully that is soon, as it's likely to me a repeat episode will occur anytime."

"Simon, we are struggling. What you ask for is improbable. But I agree that a further strike will happen anytime."

"Yes. But there is a pattern. Note: (1) the night strangulation in public places and (2) a female and (3) suspect who gets the confidence of her victim."

"We can't find someone by clearing the streets. It's the most heavily populated area in Australia?"

"OK. Point (4) we have a nocturnal person. Feels safe in the open and is as strong as a weightlifter."

"We could put some female Police Officers in vulnerable areas on their way home. It seems to fit."

"Now you are talking. Think like this killer. They will all need ready back up. Point (5) Gym workers from female only institutions. All three victims are female –correct?"

"Correct."

"The strategy must give the bitch limited opportunity, flood the public areas with female Police incognito. The public will be protected and steer clear. Is it a plan?"

"Moving towards one I would suggest. What else?"

"Have you the manpower to support this strategy?"

"Every Police Officer has been put in the hunt as a priority."

"Sergeant, do you have street surveillance reviewed?"

"We do."

"Could you bring the last three weeks here please."

"That's a shitload of vision, Simon."

"OK. But I/We must find this killer. It's personal, you see my girlfriend lives in Bronte, nearby."

"OK we will be back soon with the vision. Anything we haven't covered?"

"One more thing perhaps. Be prepared for a person disguising themselves –like a Muslim woman with a hijab. Do you have tabs on a western woman wearing something like that?"

"Shit, we never thought of that stuff. Come on Jim let's get cracking. Thanks Simon."

"You guys know that regular Police work will reduce the chances of a further incident. Check and counter check circumstance to increase our chances to catch this bitch."

The Police Officers left feeling momentum in the pursuit of this offender once more. Simon's simple plan hosted their own aim………. 'Catch this bitch'.

Simon was left depressed by this discussion. The Police for him were heroes going through this shower of misery portion of society day in and day out. It made Simon want to vomit. Then he thought of the three innocent victims and roused himself.

'What else can I do to help these guys…..THINK!'

Simon's first thoughts:

'I aspire to be Surfer Simon with a bit of Insurance work on the side –how the blazes did I end up hunting killers?'

He had some insight but seriously felt out of his depth. For the rest of that evening the Crimes Unit used their IT resources to work on reducing the suspected known offenders and the areas where they may have a repeat offence. Police patrols were increased and randomly distributed.

All parolees were interviewed in the hope someone may know something. Simon Dang spent overnight looking at CCTV footage, fast forwarding three weeks footage in six hours. It was the morning of the 31stof October. Halloween approached next night. It was now common to see both children and their parents dressed up in outfits knocking on doors all over Sydney. In Edgecliff, a lone woman dressed as a witch wandered from a park to a bus stop. The Police patrol drove by and thought that the behaviour was strange and interviewed the witch. Red faces all around as it turned out to be a school Principal walking home after a function in her school. Everyone was on alert.

Female Police were everywhere during the evening in the eastern suburbs. Simon scanned CCTV footage and became an expert after a while.

Weeks went by with no new deadly crime, the public heaved a sigh of relief and got on with the rat race. Then they had a breakthrough. A young woman had been approached in Double Bay by a "Muslim" and phoned the Crime Stoppers hotline. The Police descended on Double Bay immediately and found a woman in a nearby harbour side park with no ID. She was arrested and on interview the suspect was established as a mental health individual who had schooled in the Eastern suburbs in her youth years ago. She came across as bitter and very twisted in her responses. On analysis, Police were confident they had the suspect.

Months later, his identity private and confidential, Birthmark became an honorary Police Officer and the Governor of NSW applauded the decision –in private. Australia had unearthed an asset to the trophy cabinet – Simon Dang aka The Birthmark.

Chapter 4

Peter Maxwell was rain walking along a secondary road one Friday afternoon when he saw in the distance an unmarked, stationary, dark grey sedan with alternate flashing blue and red lights from the rear panel. Police car!

In front of the flashing car a man and a woman stood in civvies without raincoats. No uniforms, informal –shorts and runners. They were busy disengaging two cars which had smashed into each other. Two tow trucks and their drivers were nearby trying to assist as the collided vehicles blocked the road. As Peter walked by, the female undercover Police Officer went to her flashing car and extracted a high-visibility sleeveless jacket identifying her as a Police Officer. She put it on and set to work stopping the one lane of oncoming traffic behind her with an authoritative signal. The tow truck drivers moved one vehicle to a side street whilst the other really smashed up black sedan failed to start. They couldn't drive it onto the side street so they backed a tow truck car and hauled it there. Meanwhile the two undercover Police supervised and tried to clean the car debris off the road. The main road was a mess. The male Police Officer had a lanyard around his neck and a Police badge in a protective see through wallet. He nodded as Peter moved quickly past the scene. He was cool as he tried to kick car headlights and grills into the gutter.

"G'day"

Peter Maxwell wondered why the Policeman acknowledged him. Peter just smiled and went along his way, thinking that they had been forced by the crash site to reveal their unmarked car and themselves to the public. Undercover Police work, Peter thought as a normal citizen, something I know nothing about. What are they working on all day –drug dealers, computer hackers/paedophiles? One answer was not long coming.

The very next week, Peter arrived home at 16:00hrs and his wife Claudine was also home, she is a teacher on school holidays. As Peter entered the front yard there was a familiar man, he thought across the street. Peter waved hello as that man walked away down towards the shops nearby.

Peter entered the house greeting Claudine, who was in the front room. They talked for a couple of minutes then a Police van came into the street and their view driven by female Police Officer who was talking on a two way radio. This uniformed Officer parked right across the road from Peter and Claudine's house.

Now, theirs is a quiet street usually. So, both peered out the window through the blinds.

What has transpired?

Soon they witnessed the man Peter had waved hello to, sprinting back up the street followed by a man and a woman. Both were huffing on the chase. The chasers had side arms around their waist, not drawn. The Female Police Officer leading the chase.

Then the female Police Officer who had been driving the van got out and confronted the pursued man. Outnumbered he does as he is directed, kneels on a grassy patch opposite Peter and Claudine's front door. The arrested man started yelling;

"I got nothing on me. This is your mistake! Pigs!"

Guess who the chasing Police were when they arrived? The same male and female who were at the scene of the car smash that Peter had walked past. The female chasing Police Officer handcuffed the arrested man as he knelt face down, then motioned him to stand. He became unco-operative, lashing out with his feet. A crime in itself the watching Peter thought, to resist an arrest. Her male partner Officer assisted as they placed him into the back of the lock up van. Once inside the arrested man commenced to yell and protest loudly, kicking the inside of the van many times. The three Police Officers took a breather then called into their base. It was pointless to try and calm some people and they made no attempt.

"Now I know what they do. They are arresting burglars in broad daylight."

Claudine, had a blank look trying to work out what Peter was saying. A not very unusual occurrence!

Peter Maxwell wrote to the Local Area Command in Kogarah complimenting these two Officers on their publicly demonstrated work. The email from their boss was grateful as not many people will send such a message. Peter was not told much except the boss was happy with Jenny and Alex. Both work for Crime Stoppers, the NSW Police have a program to entice 'members of the public' to phone in information about unusual, criminal or disturbing situations. It often leads to follow up by uniformed Police and occasionally there will be undercover Police investigation. Last year Crime Stoppers took 322,000 calls from NSW residents. For example, in the hunt for a serial killer in the Eastern suburbs of Sydney a year ago,

Jenny was involved in the capture of a mentally disturbed woman. The capture was engineered by a man known as 'The Birthmark'. Whose eyelids only were affected by reddish discolouration from birth, this man was reputed to be a mathematical genius and clairvoyant, working for the government. Hush hush.

Jenny had heard all the Police gossip and stories of this 'background person' asset who apparently had predictive talent. An unusual nocturnal man, The Birthmark had calculated risk and bad weather damage etc. for Insurance companies in a former employment until he came to the notice of the Federal Government at an Insurance Conference.

Currently, the Police investigative staff held The Birthmark in good reputation. Jenny secretly wanted to meet him. Both Alex and Jenny had used information three months ago coming directly from The Birthmark's analysis of a drug distribution network. He had provided interpretative information after months of sleuthing with a team of detectives. The Birthmark's intuition indicated a house in Peakhurst as a front. The bust was made early morning, nailing what turned out to be an international syndicate. Seizing their contraband, tons of cash and arresting the ringleaders in simultaneous operations. That made the news. Jenny was in the background doing her job collating evidence when the news vans arrived. She tried to hide from the TV lights during the operation. Alex was briefly on also, but disappeared when the news vans rolled up. Their job completed. They were seen briefly leaving the raid but not identified.

Jenny and Alex were welcomed back on shift at Kogarah after that drug bust as 'TV' Police Officers, not very appropriate for undercover Police. The Duty Sergeant organised a morning tea and they got a phone call from The Birthmark. He congratulated them both for their part in the setup of the bust and rupturing a drug network with their research and planning. Jenny was blushing as she spoke to this reputed genius of a young man. Birthmark gave clear indication they would collaborate on his information soon as he had a few cold cases that would benefit from their methodical Policing work. Jenny was enthusiastic and Alex was very humbled when told of their now elevated reputation. Birthmark got the resources he wanted in any investigation. He had powerful friends like Police Commissioner Billy Mason, but Alex and Jenny were not aware. For the moment they returned to Crime Stoppers. But their work life had taken a turn.

Three days later they sat drinking coffee and looking out to sea. The sun shone on the water. In the lack of wind, they moved out of the car to stretch and enjoy this sunshine. It was idyllic and they started to yawn despite the caffeine. This was a burglar incident free day, so far. Then they heard the two way break the silence and got back to the car. There was a message to phone the Birthmark and the number where they could reach him. Alex dialled and identified himself, switching the phone to speaker for Jenny.

"Hello to you both, this is Simon Dang. I am interested in gaining your assistance in a cold case on my list. Are you two busy presently? My boss is your boss and has encouraged me to discuss some of my work. My role is unconventional –I can fill you in when we meet."

"Yes, sir. Simon, we are having coffee in the car looking out at Botany Bay."

"No surf there. Come to Maroubra and see a glorious two metre break. I have been surfing early this morning. How are you both?"

Jenny spoke up;

"Simon, we are being well treated after that recent drug bust. The top cops are smiling for once."

"It won't last, Jennifer. Or is it Jenny? I do have official status. Please check when you return to base. Your local Command Superintendent Pattison has been informed. This is all blessed from above."

"Jenny is fine. Alex is also nodding. We want to assist in any way."

"OK. We then move onto this cold case. You will need to take this specific request down in writing. There is a 'lifer' inmate, I believe he can be implicated in a series of sexual assaults twenty-five years ago. Thing is, there is little evidence except the transcripts of three of the four victims. I find a pattern. Even if I am wrong, there is a need for you to examine the statements of one Ronald Winthrop –W.I.N.T.H.R.O.P currently in Long Bay Goal. Do you need the date of birth?"

Alex was madly writing and shook his head.

"No. We can look it up. Let me repeat, the statements of a current lifer Ronald Winthrop to be examined for any evidence that we can implicate him in serial sexual assaults-over what period?"

"Hang on. 1981 to 1995. Otherwise enjoy your day. I will hear from you. Meticulous please."

"Yes Simon. We are on it."

They phoned the boss at Kogarah and he confirmed these special duties. He informed them that he would contact Long Bay to set up co-operation with the Corrective Services staff.

"Any assistance will be forthcoming from this command."

They divested themselves of their current workload back in Kogarah, then commenced a computer search. Followed by records management and a two-day trawl through charge sheets and every bit of information/interrogation of Ronald Winthrop. They drew some conclusions;

"Four attacks Alex in four close-ish northern suburbs. The victims gave similar detail and descriptions, similar versions of the attacks. Ronald Winthrop's account of his whereabouts is thin and sketchy. But there is no crime scene evidence, no DNA testing or suspects arrested at that time as Ronald Winthrop had been locked up for murder. I wonder what Simon can see? Have we overlooked something?"

"We need to present this to the Detectives for their scrutiny. Let's do the summary and attach the request from Birthmark with what we have and see if we can't nail Ronald for these assaults."

The Detectives later agreed with their findings despite the intervening years. The Birthmark was consulted again and his intuition into the mind of Ronald Winthrop suggested that he had never been interviewed about the assaults. Therefore, Simon encouraged the Officers to now request an interview with Ronald Winthrop in Long Bay. Ronald Winthrop proved to a chronically sick man these days. After those interviews a vulnerable Ronald admitted to being involved and gave a statement. He was charged and pleaded guilty. The courts would deal with Ronald should he survive his illness. Jenny and Alex doubted it, but their first cold case was finalised. Victims and their families were informed and a ground swell of appreciation for the Police department followed.

Chapter 5

J enny and Alex found themselves promoted, now they knew why The Birthmark was held in high regard. Simon Dang was on the phone to congratulate them. Next day, Simon spent his early morning at Maroubra-north end, surfing. When he arrived home there were two young people on the veranda holdinga package. They were about to knock on his private entrance.

"Hello. I am Simon Dang."

"Alex Sutcliffe and this is Jenny Dolan. We hoped to thank you but you are not home."

Alex picked up the package. Simon was slight and wiry, he smiled and accepted the gift in one hand. Jenny was giggling, they had bought Simon a way too big Hawaiian shirt.

"Thanks, but what is this for?"

He wore a towel around his waist and a T shirt only, he carried a surfboard which he put down on the veranda and shook hands. Opening the package he tried on the shirt which hung to mid thighs. They all got a laugh out of that.

"I will treasure this."

For Simon this was an unexpected pleasure, at the end of his 'day'. Simon wore a cap over his longish hair and when he removed it, he placed it on the fin of the surfboard. Both Jenny and Alex were smiling and noticed immediately Simon's eyelids covered in a reddish tissue –his birthmark. When shaking hands,

Simon had immediately felt both of their 'energy'. He could do this without effort. Both of these Officers presented as genuine and solid. Simon fished the key from the pot plant.

"Come in please. Let me get a cup of tea going. I can offer vegemite on toast also."

They spent two hours in Simon's home office, going away impressed with him. He was a winner. You can't fool the Police. Positivity and goodness were evident to them both and a brain to boot. They discussed many subjects and realised why the Australian Government had Simon in a Consult role as well as helping the various Police forces around the nation. His security clearance must be unbelievable. They realised how lucky they were to work with him and to be given direct access to him and his home.

"I am at a disadvantage as I must work at night. I am sensitive to sunlight but chance my arm early morning in the sea, with no great effect. Are you two happy to continue to work with me? I have a pile of requests outstanding. Currently many important issues are untouched as I work alone. If you two are prepared to work with a nocturnal man then we could maybe reduce this pile of outstanding work. Your bosses will do whatever is requested by my 'office'."

Simon laughed.

"Why us? If I might be so bold."

"Good question. Up front you two are a good team, this is proven. You have the advantage of being capable in Police work and the energy to get things done. Your boss at Kogarah has supported you both. Plus as

I hope, we will trust each other and make progress with my requests. Methodical investigation and attention to detail is required."

Jenny looked quickly at Alex who nodded. It was enough. Jenny and Alex agreed to the proposal immediately. This was task force work, leg work that was in fact a radical change for their previous roles. They both quietly relished this opportunity.

Days later they were both surprised to be asked to attend a meeting with the Police Commissioner in the city. Serious shit. They had to find uniforms rarely worn and both tried to look sharp as they waited outside his office in the city. Police Commissioner Billy Mason appeared suddenly.

"You two look like Coppers who have never worn those uniforms. Maybe I should send you both back to the Academy for rehab."

Alex and Jenny smiled and stood to attention in silence.

"OK. Come in. This Birthmark bloke –Simon Dang, is something special. The Government of Australia recognises it, the Governor of NSW respects him and I sure as shit agree with them both. You are being assigned as NSW Police Officers to play a critical role to support the Birthmark. You will remain as Police Officers working under Simon's direction. I expect that when you take this opportunity, that the both of you will be involved with a work tempo unknown to us normal Coppers. Any questions?"

"Sir. Can we have access to your office under these roles?"

"Yes, Yes and Yes. In fact, I expect to be fully informed by the pair of you on a month to month basis of your operations and how our staff can assist. The monthly report will include enough detail to inform me but not overwhelm my feeble mind. Obviously it must be confidential to this office so you will report in person. Your records so far are exemplary. Keep it that way and I will move heaven and earth to support you. Are we clear?"

They both tried to salute and the Police Commissioner laughed in their faces, genuinely amused.

"Get out of my office! Go and catch some criminals."

The stage was set. Next day they visited their new boss early. He was as usual was in a wetsuit and carrying a surfboard. He made tea and gave them both a summary of his workload that he had reviewed overnight. It was more than daunting. During their twenty minute meet, more requests hit Simon's secure e-mail on a PC behind him.

"I. We are a victim of success. They all now think that we can solve all their issues. Incorrect. Believe me when I say we are limited. Remember that. We must prioritise our activity. There must be room for emergency and high level requests. The PM's office does get in contact, The NSW Governor is a confidant so be prepared. It may prove a shock to you both so take copious notes. Nothing you both do can be discussed with a third party, excluding the Commissioner and the Feds. You will soon get to know the important players. I have informed the leaders that we have joined forces and you must win their trust. Then we will move mountains. Stay calm and we will get on with it. Your holidays are already looking good I'm sure. My home, by the way, is heavily protected. The day you presented yourselves and with my present is all on CCTV. There are regular watchers who can be relied on in an emergency. Otherwise forget you know about them. Act like normal undercover Cops."

Simon laughed at the confused looks. Alex and Jenny had been delivered into a rarefied atmosphere and were shell shocked but raring to get on with it.

Alex and Jenny took their lists and the brief instructions and headed for the office set aside for Simon in a nearby town centre building. Simon had never worked from that location, preferring to stay at home. It was private and ideally comfortable. They set themselves up and examined their lists for the day, then re-opened the archived brown and bruised boxes of files to review the first items on their lists. The evidence together with their database would be essential; Simon had directed the two resources to find any link. Match some characteristics and track it all down. Both Alex and Jenny, of course were aware that most detective work was routine, patient checking. Laborious but essential.

Chapter 6

"Shit, Jenny. What have we let ourselves in for? This is tedious work, like looking for missing persons after six months and beyond."

"It's only a list. Are they the same? No. Shit, my list is different!"

"OK. We have to be thorough and get a handle on what he really wants from us. An operational arm –yes. A research arm-yes. There is nothing here that's beyond us, it's just a bloody long list."

"Coffee? Let's get some fresh air and think this through."

"He said prioritise. OK with that but.........my list. Hang on, Simon has already put things in a priority list. Some of this stuff may be straightforward."

They walked and bought coffee, in a shop where a man and his magnificent Doberman dog sat by his side on a pavement table. He looked to be enjoying the sunshine and morning expresso. On the return with coffee, they were ready to commence.

"Let's work through it. Start with your list, what's number one?"

"Item one is a forecast of rainfall to fill the Darling River. Currently it's dry. Estimated at completely dry of its former self. Many people are suffering in the drought out there."

"How can we handle that? Are we supposed to turn the rivers around so that they don't run out to sea?"

"Phone call to the Bureau of Meteorology and examination of the past records. Should be on the net, let's look it up. Hang on, what about the Water board-bound to have info."

In a little time they came up with the known information. They wrote a summary and set it aside for Simon. Only God knows when it is going to rain. Item 2, they then worked on. During that day they gained an idea of the workload on Simon. They did their best to provide information to many items on the respective lists and left it for him. Then they went home not knowing if it was enough. Next day at dawn it was raining. Simon opened the door and ushered them in.

"OK. Some good stuff to assist. Predictive work I will handle, I should not have put the weather forecast on your list. Apologies. Otherwise very helpful. Today is a shorter list for both of you, then I need research on a job just come in. If we can keep up to date on any of our work requests I will be so grateful. You two being here is a relief for me. Thanks."

They both examined their lists and were astounded with one item.

'Please go to Centennial Park and walk/run around for an hour. This is mandatory. For your health.'

It seemed like a reward. Then the Federal Government ASIO office rang, Cyber security had indicated they were under Chinese attack on some Government platforms. All their preparation was in place, they simply wanted to have Simon look over it. All three reviewed the 'eyes only' status. Simon was in his element and phoned after a while.

"Jim. I have found no breach. Is it consistent with your examination?"

"Hi Simon. Yes. We are confident. The Americans are firing warnings at us every hour. They have a definite issue with some of the Chinese military stuff."

"OK. I am happy to sign off with you. See ya."

Simon shook his head, the international work took the working day to 24 hours. He would never get to the beach!

Jenny announced she was getting married to Thomas, her soldier and sought leave for a 3 week period to holiday in North Queensland. Simon was happy for her. He wished her and her husband well. It brought home his isolation from everyone except the surfers early morning in Maroubra. Alex was already in a relationship with a lady he called Nic (Nicole). He was happy to work solo as it would be difficult to bring someone into their confidential operation for three weeks. During the third week an unusual situation unfolded.

"OK Alex, we have a situation with a siege in Newcastle. A man has locked up his three wives –that's 3 wives and threatens to burn the house down. Police are on the scene but they want a predictive on this man...Joshua Wetherill. DOB 22/11/1978. Can you give me as much info as you can ASAP?"

"Yes I will try. Give me a few minutes."

An hour later Alex put his notes in the computer;

"Simon, alternative religious person (3 wives). Well known to Police. No domestic violence stats.

Involved with stealing cattle and sheep in the past. Runs a backyard/ roadside green business –honey, sun dried tomatoes, etc. No recent events. No indication of his reasons for threats to the family. Police on the scene currently say he has released two children from the house. They are in good shape."

Simon read and rang the Officer on site.

"Simon Dang here. What can you tell me?"

"Hello Simon. I am Wilson, from the Riot squad, your advice would be welcome. This man's refusing to talk to us and is not listening. Keeps waving a rifle in the window. We have no idea if he's mental or simply frustrated."

"Frustrated. He is not likely to kill anyone. Get your negotiators talking to him and then storm the castle. End this thing before he does any irrational stuff."

The Police Officer, Wilson stared at the phone and mouthed 'storm the castle' to himself. He then got the negotiators talking again and moved with the 'Special Tactics Command Police' on the house from three other sides. They arrested the man without a shot being fired and the Area Commander wrote his report while the TV news congratulated the NSW Police.

The Police Commissioner sat at home and smiled. He thought to himself whoever invented Simon Dang deserved a medal.

A week later Jenny returned to a burned out Alex and a birth marked boss who needed a day off. A blissfully happy Jenny gave them 'no work' orders.

"I am holding the phone. Go. If the palace burns down I will tell you tomorrow!"

Alex and Simon ran away. Each of them enjoyed the prospect of a day to themselves as many issues had arrived on the doorstep since Jenny had wed. Jenny spent the day regaining her insight into this fabulous job that she had fallen into and finalising paperwork for Alex. She had time to contemplate her new husband bound for Townsville and army projects and already wished he was coming home.

One news item disturbed Jenny. News arrived of another body found in the National Park south of Sutherland. It was not far from a fire trail used by the SES and the dismembered corpse was buried in a shallow grave that had been dug up by native animals and black crows. Forensic experts were working on the post mortem currently. Jenny made a follow up note to discuss with Simon. The rest of the day zipped by with routine tasks. Jenny, before she left composed an outstanding list for herself and Alex to commence next day after the morning 'prayer' meeting with Simon to prioritise their work.

Chapter 7

Walter 'Lucky' Lermontov stared out of the window of the coffee shop three suburbs away on the fringe of the city. He liked to watch the females all dressed up heading to work in the CBD. Lucky moved a hand across his unshaven face and sniffed. He needed a shower after his night activity. Sooner rather than later, so he finished his expresso and put his cap on, stepping into the rat race that was the street. Lucky was a contract 'hit man' with the strength of a larger man. Lucky could blend in, follow a target and time his assault like the former SAS regiment man he was. Last week he had chopped up that 'hit' who had been targeted by his contact as a 'bludger who will not pay his debts'. Directive had been to 'Finalise him'....

Lucky had enjoyed the task such was his temperament. Stalking the hit, disposing of the body all in a night's work. He may have acted like a predator but Lucky knew he was not a psychopath –or was he?

There was no emotion, certainly no remorse. It was the job to be cruel, calculating and aggressive, after all it had happened to Lucky himself throughout his childhood. The absence of love, he felt like a loser after plainly doing nothing wrong. The pain and anger builds up to a strike force –that's a breeding ground for people like Walter Lermontov.

Lucky hoped there would be more contracts like recently as the victims get what they deserve. Too easy and it pays. No rat race employment for this little black duck who in reality was demonstrating psychopathic traits. The call sign 'black duck' was Lucky's favourite.

Lucky was busy in his quiet time setting up safe havens and identity 'transfers' should he be detected and pursued. It was all necessary to have safe haven and escape plans in place. His type of employment demanded it. He also enjoyed keeping very fit and strong as this was vital to his survival.

Years ago the army had given instruction on how to put a charge on something and blow it up. Explosives was not everyday knowledge and Lucky had absorbed it all well. The military service had been his salvation with a typical adolescence, in and out of Institutions he was on the road to more and more goal time. The army had given him discipline, learning but also accommodation and a clean lifestyle. Plus he got to shoot and blow things up on occasion. He was mobilised to Afghanistan in 1985. It was a whole other world and Lucky was wounded in the leg. He recovered, then made every measure a target for himself and was promoted but not loved by his company of soldiers. Lucky was unable to run very far when he returned to the Black Sea.

"Hi team."

Simon stood with surfboard in hand.

"Sorry. I am late for you, the sea is really pumping. Anyway come in."

Alex and Jenny walked in for the morning briefing. Both were jumpy but waited on Simon with his tea ceremony.

"Simon, I am worried about this body in the Royal National Park, the victim has been chopped up like a Nepalese funeral ceremony to feed the vultures. Who could do that?"

"Oh dear. What have we got so far?"

"Forensic examination. Dr Adler did give me an indication it was a hit! What a surprise. We are at square one on this. Keep you posted."

"What is on our agenda today boss?"

Alex asked.

"Finish off what is on your lists. Clear the deck. I am having premonitions of big tasks for all of us."

Silence from the 'Coppers'. They duly left to carry out their orders, but of course wondering what Simon had hinted at? There followed two days of mopping up and the satisfaction that goes with that, then the inevitable report to the Commissioner.

"What are you two reprobates up to? I am hearing nothing and guess what- My sources are impeccable!"

"Sir, we have cleared our current workload. There may be some delay now assisting your departments but Simon has instructed we 'clear the deck'"

"Good on Simon."

"Sir, the chopped up body in the National Park in Sutherland has captured his interest."

"That's good news to my office here. Anything else?"

"We are exhausted Sir. This bloke –The Birthmark never stops."

"Understand. Let me emphasise what an asset he is to our country. I urge you to see it from our viewpoint. You are working with a man possessed of skills unprecedented in my thirty five years' service as a Police Officer. There will always be a need for this special work. Keep me informed-I am pleased with your hit rate on 'my' outstanding worklist. Congratulations."

Alex and Jenny looked at each other in dismay, then left.

Lucky had a phone message to respond to that evening. He was at the football encouraging his team, South Sydney to play to their skills. It was a local grudge match with Eastern Suburbs and the heat was on. Lucky looked at his phone and decided to wait till half time as the woman sitting nearby in his row had wonderful legs and they were enough distraction from the football. Lucky messaged at half time;

'Black duck. The message?'

Immediately the reply was apparent;

'Post office box tomorrow at 10:00. I have an errand.'

Lucky took his Doberman, Boris, with him next day. Boris was a magnificent deep chested black and tan, they looked like any other dog walker collecting his mail, except there was no lead on Boris. When his master stopped, Boris stopped. Lucky collected his post then headed for the beach promenade via the coffee shop. Lucky did not tie up Boris, merely pointed to the doorway. Boris sat on the footpath looking at the Cafe door waiting for Lucky to re-appear. Anyone approaching Boris would see his teeth and a low growl. No one patted Boris on the head, except Lucky.

There was privacy on a beach bench to open his mail. Boris sat next to his feet like the guard dog he was, looking out to sea not distracted by birds or people.

The Coroner examining the chopped up remains from the National park crime site reported bite marks on the extremities of both legs and one arm. The other arm mangled. The bites resembled the jaw outline of a 'large canine'. Other than that, the victim was murdered with a stiletto knife, the killer knew exactly where to strike. No prints were lifted and x-rays confirmed normal height (170cm approx.) and weight of the man (80 -85kg). No tattoos or other remarkable appearance.

death from rectal temperatures could have been a week to ten days. The man was known to Police. Investigations were underway.

"Simon here"

"Detective Hadley from Sutherland Police, sir. Can I have a moment regarding the body found in the Royal National park recently?"

"Go ahead Detective."

"We are still unsure why the body was mutilated. Post death why would you murder someone then go to all the trouble to cut their corpse up? We know the victim, a considerable offender who owed money all over town."

"Seems extreme doesn't it, and it was done at another location. The clean-up would be extensive. I think the killer is trying hard to throw us off. We may have a very sick and sadistic murderer. Dog bites probably mean there was a chase. The effect of the body in pieces spells a warning to others I am guessing. Loan sharks expect interest on their loans."

"Contract hit, sir?"

"You got it in one."

"Thanks sir. We will concentrate on our known hitmen through the normal channels. Any other suggestions, Sir."

"Top end of town, Detective, or Organised crime. Who can afford to make an example like this? Hitmen are expensive. Especially the ones with a psychosis who could pull this deed off. Also were there canine hairs on the body –the chase and a struggle? Perhaps dog faeces at the site?"

"Not to my knowledge, we will check that and on a man with a dog. Thank you, sir."

Simon made note of the contact with Detective Hadley and turned to the surf report forecast for tomorrow early.

Alex and Jenny were on Maroubra beach walking early next day. Simon in a pack of surfers fighting for the wave positions. He saw them and cut short his recreation and paddled in. Simon put down his surfboard not welcoming the intrusion into his time.

"Sorry Simon. We have been notified overnight of another grisly murder. A woman, identified as Denise Bray found by a jogger, attached to one of the stanchion of the Iron Cove Bridge. Half drowned and knifed, that's all at the moment. We wouldn't be here except the Commissioner demands a quick find. Apparently he knew the family. He was also raving about a crime wave."

"Jealous husband, you think?"

Simon was relaxed and towelling down.

"Knifed expertly. I refer to the detective on the scene overnight. And bite marks on the left ankle."

"Oh dear, another hit. Let's get moving."

They rescheduled all other work and stayed at Simon's house as the calls came in from Detectives charged with the investigation after breakfast. This was now their priority. Jenny collated the known information about Denise Bray and her family as Alex and Simon swotted about a contract killer with a dog making big money overnight.

"He's punished the woman by (a) nearly drowning her then (b) knifed her and (c) leaving her in a public place on display as it were."

"We've got a professional male with a savage dog that he lets chase down the victim –then kills them under direction? Who could be funding these crimes?"

"Where does one learn how to kill with a knife-SAS? The Balkans? Teaching a dog to bring down a person is also not common. Get on the phone to Detective Hadley at Sutherland, he was investigating contract killers. Let's see where we are up to. Also the Iron Cove bridge site, maybe he's made a mistake. Left a print on the stanchion or something. He may have touched it placing the rope. The crime scene team have got to find us something, footmarks in the mud all over that place. Did we get footmarks from the National Park? It will confirm our man if they match. And he must be using a van, tyre tracks as well. CCTV vision from the approaches to the Iron Cove Bridge-we must have it. Same dog hairs at both sites will be evidence."

Simon exhaled, he was no longer relaxed. He phoned a friend in National Security in Canberra. Described their search and was given immediate support. Information would be forthcoming as they used the resources to track down any possible suspects. Simon could do no more until the Detectives and the Feds came through. Simon did recall however that when CCTV was introduced into the city centre there were protests about privacy issues. Now the public feels more secure. Its smart proactive policing.

Walter 'Lucky' Lermontov ticked off his list as the expresso in front of him cooled a bit. Things were the opposite of disappointing. Is the word appointing? English can be so confusing. The list was making him satisfied, as he was today, one step closer to retirement. The contract work had hit a peak and Lucky was now on the prowl for some entertainment.

A day later, Lucky's phone vibrated with a message. It was a picture of his homeland near the Black sea and wild (black) ducks. He knew who had sent it and left his coffee to make a call. A colleague from his Military service contacting him about a meeting they need to have.

"Walter Lermontov, you solitary bastard, why have you not contacted me? Is it five or ten years? We must find a bar and reunite, my friend."

"Not long enough, Turkish swine, Altan! Why would I want to drink beer with you?"

There was tons of laughter at the other end. They both composed themselves delighted to be in contact again.

"When can we meet? Where? It's been a long time."

Good judgement comes from experience. The Black duck wanted to meet his old friend and drink beer.

No work!

"OK we got the van and the time last night. CCTV shows vision of a tall man with a large dog (we knew that) and a woman (the victim). That puts the players in the vicinity of the crime scene and the Van plates and ID are routine, it's a rental. We are making progress and the evidence is mounting. We lifted a fingerprint from the bridge stanchion up high. Thank God. They are running it now to find a match."

The phone rang mid sentence.

"Simon here. Yes Commissioner we have progress! Looks like a former SAS soldier contract killer, maybe not one of ours. The expert use of a knife is the definitive weapon here. We have a list and are investigating which SAS force uses Dobermans as their gun dogs. Turkey perhaps —one of the Balkan nations. Can we get them to co-operate perhaps with their former elite military records?"

"Yes. Criminal requests are usually supported between Embassies. I will get right on it with the Turkish and Russian authorities. Is it Hadley from Sutherland handling this?"

"Yes sir. He is the man I have spoken to."

The Birthmark

Jenny and Alex forced themselves to review and wait. They could not plan without solid evidence passing through the layers of experts to launch an arrest. They decided to go over the whole situation on a white board. The plates had been easy though and traced to a hire company. The subsequent request to them was expedited and the name and details of a client named 'Jim Carrey' were revealed. No help really. They investigated an address from the licence and turned up a happy family. Strike out. Dead end. It is not easy to catch a SAS killer who has gone off the rails. A day passed.

The investigation developed some momentum again with a match of the print on Interpol. Walter Lermontov's name provided a whole new avenue of investigation. The hunt was on. Everyone amped up their search now for Walter Lermontov in Sydney. Every person with that surname was investigated. There were twenty three. An old photo was released and the warrant was issued and the address matched the 'Jim Carrey' who had hired the van. Standard policing.

They involved every Police officer in Sydney and mentioned the dog. Do not approach under any circumstances but report any siting. No one was home at the given address of 'Jim Carrey'. They would have to wait. The unmarked car of Jenny and Alex parked down the road watching the comings and goings at the apartment in Edgecliff. Matched by a second undercover car at the other end of the street.

Detectives in the background continued to build a case with the evidence so accumulated. It was becoming obvious to them that Mr. Lermontov was the man of interest. The worry now was where was Mr. Lermontov?

No one could know that Walter Lermontov was drinking beer with his friend, Altan from the past. It proved a long wait. The Black Duck Lermontov was stung and shattered. Reunion after a dinner and a pub crawl had been the tonic for his circumstance. As the night progressed and the stories reached back into his memory Lucky's awareness became sub optimal.

45

The Police surprised him at his front door at 04:00 hrs and there were 'hundreds of them'. Walter Lermontov was arrested after a struggle and charged with murder (x2) subsequent to interview at Police headquarters. Walter, the black duck, refused to co-operate with the interviewing Police. They had no statement as Walter was incoherent. They locked him up to sleep it off. Police had derived evidence that he was a contract assassin and his profile matched that evidence as more information came through from overseas damning his activity with the skills he possessed. The only thing missing was the Doberman.

Apparently a neighbour was looking after the dog. The Police visiting that neighbour had big issues getting a sample of hair from Boris. Finally the Dog Squad Vet had to tranquilise Boris after the neighbour handed the dog to him. Boris had put up more of a fight than his master. The vet examined the anesthetized Boris and recognised a superior animal. He thought a potential recruit for the Dog squad.

Simon Dang's team had pulled off another great piece of work in helping to capture a contract killer. Birthmark had brought someone like Lermontov to justice swiftly.

Chapter 8

G reg Kelly was hot and waved his arms in boredom, fielding at fine leg on a cricket field called Tasker Park, he exhaled to relax. This game, played adjacent to the Cooks River was 'lost' and he was counting the minutes till the opposition's innings came to completion. Greg's team had run out of time, his thoughts whilst fielding moved to motorcycle parts and the aspiration of ownership of a new and powerful motorcycle. At sixteen years, Greg was ready (he thought) for the senior grades of the game of cricket, however the competition for selection was fierce. Greg's talents were comprehensive but he feared that he would be overlooked even though he had worked hard on his skills. Greg was a loner and never understood the work of 'political supporters' required to ensure selection into Grade cricket. Greg's main supporter was his Mum at home.

Today Greg's team decided at the completion of their lost game to swim afterwards and relax at one of the players' homes. Greg liked the team but had other plans besides swimming. Greg said farewell and headed home. He knew that he would not be missed at the home and pool of one of the rich guys in the team.

Greg was friendly but kept a low social profile, his personality did not require recognition.

Greg on arriving home, greeted his smoking Mother with a squeeze and hustled her gently sideways out from the kitchen bench to make a sandwich. His Mother was indulgent and loved her quiet unassuming son. Marie Kelly, however had made sure of one thing with Greg growing up. When he was old enough,

Marie had a passion for and loved to read Australian writing to him. Banjo Paterson and Henry Lawson, her favourites as they wrote of the bush and real Australians. Banjo's 'The Man from Snowy River' Marie could recite in her sleep. 'The Loaded Dog' by Henry Lawson made Marie laugh. Marie would often throw a 'line' from those authors' writings into conversation with Greg, such was her passion. Greg, of course, became a fan. He loved his Mum.

Today, post cricket, Greg left the kitchen with his sandwich late lunch and Marie didn't have to ask where he was headed. Greg also filched a can of beer from his Father's fridge whilst he sat in the garage and stared at the old restored BSA Bantam motorbike now his own, chewing on the ham, tomato and cheese.

The BSA had been a challenge, but the rebuild was complete now and Greg felt accomplishment. He had learned a lot from this project. This was very satisfactory to Greg. Finishing eating, he found some decent rags and set about cleaning all the shiny bits of the restored motorbike. He painted the tyres black and oiled the chain. This bike would now pass registration for the road for sure. Greg knew the engine was clean as a whistle on the inside and wanted to add some shine to his project, it was a focus of all the work he had done to bring this motorcycle back to close to an original condition. Greg had offers to buy it but it was his first achievement and declined all approaches.

Tension gone with the touch up cleaning, Greg opened the garage door for a bit of a breeze in the coming darkness. He looked beyond his driveway towards the Cooks River (more like a concrete canal) to an overgrown riverbank wilderness at the end of the street. This shoreline which provided a testing ground for his unregistered BSA.

Greg prepared for a 'run' with his restored and clean motorcycle. His attention was diverted then to a single headlamp which lit up the road to his right. Recognising the deep engine sound of a Harley-Davidson coming his way Greg stood driveway silent and watched. The large bike turned into Greg's drive and stopped. He had a visitor. The rider parked his motorcycle and took off his helmet to unzip his leather jacket. Removing his helmet, he turned off his bike and moved down the driveway to Greg.

"How ya going?"

This tall man in full leathers extended his hand. Greg wiped his greasy right hand on his overalls and thought his Mother would not be pleased. Stuttering a little;

"What can I do for you?"

"Shannon Croft. I live 'up the road' and have seen you working on that old bike. Is it your hobby?"

Greg was surprised by the direct enquiry. An unusual encounter.

"Yes. You want to see it?"

"A man of few words. I like that –Greg Kelly isn't it?"

"Yes, Shannon. How would you know that?"

"My brother's in your cricket team. Alan Croft. Greg –you guys got beat today!"

Shannon smiled briefly. Shannon had perfect teeth and was well groomed as Greg looked beyond him to the large Harley-Davidson Wide Glide in his driveway. Maybe 2014 model, Greg thought. A beauty. Greg moved closer and confirmed the model. He was correct. The darkness in that driveway was increasing.

"Can you give me an opinion Greg? My bike starts OK but when idling at the lights in traffic it can give a hiccup. Oh, good grief this old BSA is a beauty – you did all this?"

Greg was all concentration, silent and listening. He was pleased with the compliment but thought now only about why Shannon Croft had come to see him.

"Can you roll your Wide Glide inside? We are losing the light in the driveway."

Shannon did as asked and turned to see Greg on his haunches squatting to examine the bike under the petrol tank with a torch. Greg was forthright.

"Harleys are very different. You should take it to a mechanic who has had the special training."

Shannon shrugged in encouragement and started to assess Greg, who moved to get tools and open the petrol tank and look closely at the fuel lines. The petrol tank was thankfully low on fuel. Greg got a small, clean glass jar. He looped a small rope around the rim and lowered it into the tank to scoop some fuel from the bottom. No mean feat. Holding the retrieved fuel up to the light there was tiny particulate matter present. It should not be present in the tank and they both realised that. Greg showed it to Shannon, then poured it down the sink.

"See the floaties. I bet they are in your fuel line and will clog up your connections. Simple."

Greg got some tools from a metal case nearby and disconnected a fuel line and drained the petrol into the jar. Same result, same contamination.

"Are you using Premium fuel on your premium bike?"

"Nah, too expensive."

"The low grades of fuel, Like E10, will build up and when idling can cause that 'hiccup' –as you describe. Engine efficiency is optimal with higher grade fuels."

"No shit. Greg I am impressed. How can I flush out this particulate matter?"

"Have to take it to an expert to get it all out. How long have you had this model?"

"Since new two years ago, my friend. By the way, our bike club could use a bloke like you."

Greg was immediately interested but waited for more information.

"A bunch of enthusiasts with a wide variety of backgrounds talking about bikes."

"Shannon, I am still at school and without a licence to ride yet."

"Don't matter. Your skills will flourish and you will enjoy the group. No pressure."

Greg stared at Shannon.

"I will think about it, thanks."

Chapter 9

At Police headquarters in Sydney, NSW Police Commissioner Billy Mason came from behind his desk to welcome Simon Dang, aka The Birthmark. Simon had just worked through the night with his caseload and Billy was very aware of that and the value of this man. Simon was everyone's secret weapon.

"Let's have tea. I will be frank –thanks for coming by the way. I am under pressure, Simon. Sorry to bring a night owl like you here at this time but it is imperative we talk."

"I'm listening, Sir."

This gladdened the heart of Billy Mason that this very talented young man called him 'Sir'. He smiled at the respect, then continued with mutual good feelings. Billy tried to speak in equal terms with Simon.

"These bikie gang punks are taking the NSW Government to the High Court presently for the SCPO Act. As you know these laws are aimed at controlling alleged criminal activity by bikie gangs. Lawyers for the Rebels Bike gang argue that....Let me read it....'The SCPO Act' erects in substance an alternative criminal justice system, significantly more favourable to the state and less favourable to accused persons'...."

The Commissioner continued.

"I have been instructed to lay off the Gangs while the case is heard. Guess what, the buggers have gone on a recruitment drive while the NSW Police have their hands tied. Simon, their activity has multiplied."

Simon politely waited for the Commissioner to finish;

"These are the laws of collaboration with known criminals and public meetings?"

"Yes. The Rebels lawyers contend that it is unconstitutional, even though it is designed to protect the public. Anyway that aside I want to ask you for some advice while the Raptor squad that targets the bikies is on 'holidays'."

Simon was honest and clear.

"I suggest that we reveal to the public the essence of present day goals like Long Bay in Sydney, with unhealthy, tattooed individuals incarcerated in our institutions because of their bikie gang criminal activity.

The gangs promise all, including young recruits a blast of fun times, fast money, easy life etc. The truth, we agree, is very different. Expose them for all their suspected criminal aspirations. You don't have to prove a thing. Advertising to every citizen the warts and all activity of a gang member. Maybe shut down their websites? Can we do that?"

"I'll get the legal people on it and talk to the Minister. It will augment our undercover work. Thanks."

"How about my undercover duo-Jenny and Alex, do you need their help?"

"Yes. I'm sure they will have ideas as well. Can you spare them a couple of days?"

"Of course. They will report to you this morning. Currently the workload is medium priority only."

The undercover duo, Jenny Dolan and Alex Sutcliffe were in the gym 'working'. Working out, they were participating in a gym class, a morning 'fitness crusher' class to suss out a woman who was suspected of being drug mule. Circumstantial associations needed to be checked first hand. Patient the pair had to be, but they got a workout and followed the suspect. Turned out she went straight to work, which they confirmed with the records computer in their car. So they made notes into a file and returned to their 'office' up the road from Simon Dang's home. Simon by now, they thought, would be sleeping.

Greg Kelly finished school in that next year and wondered what to do with his life. He certainly didn't want to go to university but would like a learning job. He enrolled in a trade class as a mechanic to pursue his passion for motorcycles. This acceptance to the course pleased him no end.

One Saturday in December post enrolment for the next semester, Greg was with a Bike Club member walking past the local Pub parking area when they saw a man struggling to kick-start his older Harley-Davidson motorbike. Greg approached the frustrated man.

"I can help, perhaps if you clutch start it you'll be able to get it to a mechanic."

"Never done a clutch start. Key start always works."

The man waited, then tried again. Greg waited.

"If you let me handle it, I can get it started for you."

The frustrated man was thinking to himself....'I'm not gonna let this kid touch my bike!'

Greg's Bike Club friend spoke up;

"I can vouch for him. Greg here is our Motorcycle Club Mechanic."

The man backed away and signalled for Greg to try and start his motorbike. Greg moved quickly and first put the bike into neutral gear, then turned on the ignition, he got the bike rolling in the car park then kicked into second gear and gunned the throttle. The motorbike burst into life and Greg did a swift tight circle to bring the throbbing bike back to the two men waiting. Greg got off, kicked the stand down and walked away. The frustrated man smiled and yelled his thanks.

There was another man who had witnessed this expert display. A Rebel bikie gang club member carrying his groceries in normal clothes. He memorised the young man's face who had just clutch started a motorbike and controlled the tight circular return in a crowded car park and made it look easy.

Months later the Rebels tracked Greg Kelly down and made him an offer of an apprenticeship in one of their repair shops. It was a short discussion for both parties. Greg wondered about 'out of the blue' circumstance but resolved to work hard in an area of work that was his passion. Greg's Mother Marie was delighted he had found employment. Life can surprise you. Greg found his niche. The Rebels had a success going on downstairs in a building that housed a busy 'Repair and New Motorcycle' sales as they laundered money from drug sales upstairs through the business.

In time the Rebel bosses had to open another shop to try and deflect attention from their legitimate repair shop. Greg Kelly was handling all the work they could throw at him in that the legitimate business of repairs and sales. He never asked what was going on upstairs.

Greg Kelly was introduced by his senior boss, Joe and mentor to a social whirl once he established his role in the repair shop. Business was brisk and the people traffic coming and going was considerable. Parties.

Horse Race meetings. There were social events weekly he could attend. Greg chose to study and learn. The curve was steep with the Harley-Davidson bikes he got to work on and Joe was enthusiastic in nurturing Greg's skills as he found in Greg - substance. Greg learnt how to deal with people in general, even the daily big and tough queue jumpers who used their 'standover tactics' to try and get their bikes attended to quicker. Greg was passively resistant, simply expressing confusion at the state of their bikes and asked them to be patient. He showed the door to a few and word got around. The Rebel bosses upstairs were delighted with the polite but assured Greg Kelly. For Greg the feeling was mutual.

The NSW Police Bike Gang squad-*Raptor* became aware of Greg Kelly's repair shop as the greedy Rebel bosses laundered much too much money through the business. The books were examined by their investigators in a routine tax evasion investigation. Analysis over a couple of months showed the volume of money was significantly higher than similar business models available to the Tax Office. Raptor Officers prepared to raid the premises of Greg Kelly's workplace forthwith with a Court order. It happened one early morning. Alex and Jenny, undercover cops were prominent in the raid.

Their findings were astounding and arrests were made. Cash, firearms and computers were seized in a daybreak raid. It hit the press and closed down Greg's workplace that morning as he got to work. Greg Kelly was pissed off by the whole mess. Of course, Greg knew little about what had gone on upstairs, but the workshop was his niche and suddenly he was out of work. This left a bad taste in Greg's mouth as he had work to be done. He even vowed quiet vengeance.

Henry Lawson filtered through to the forefront of his depressed mind;

'So we must fly a rebel flag, as others did before us. And we must sing a rebel song and join in rebel chorus. We'll make the tyrants feel the sting O'those that they would throttle; They needn't say the fault is ours if blood should stain the wattle.'

Henry Lawson was writing about the greed of landowners and the oppression of common folk in the late 19th century. For Greg, the cycle of his short working life equalled finding a good job, ride high on your deeds, then see the bosses escorted from the premises. The business shut down with a Court order. It couldn't be true. Joe, the boss of the Repair shop was inconsolable but tried to give hope to Greg.

"Never mind, Greg. There will be another opportunity."

Marie Kelly consoled her son and was worried about his dark mood. He brightened with this advice from his adored Mother.

"Thanks Mum."

Then Greg disappeared into the garage. He had salvaged an old Harley-Davidson soft tail with his savings and was working hard to bring it back. Greg thought perhaps he could work from home and equip his Dad's garage and sell re-conditioned motorcycles. He was seething with the situation.

Jenny and Alex, The Birthmark's undercover team examined the documents and summary report of the 'Rebels Repair shop' as they called it. Sales were double to triple a similar franchise. They also investigated the employees and their background. The Accountant providing the books would be dealt with by the Tax department. His contribution was under scrutiny currently. The scramble was on big time for him.

Jenny and Alex paused with employee, one Greg Kelly-an unknown. ?normal young man without a hint of adolescent drama. Why would this person join the Rebels? They consulted with Simon Dang next day.

Perhaps they were making too many assumptions.

"Simon, we have a question about the Rebels Repair Shop. There is one young man- Greg Kelly, an apprentice in the business with a trouble free past and an attendance at his trade course that is first rate. He has exemplary marks with serious support from his Lecturers. What the hell is doing in there?"

"Interesting. These guys usually have troubled relatives and spivs working in the low paid jobs. His name again please?"

"Greg Kelly."

"I have a theory. You want to hear it? OK. I think that is one lucky young man to be removed from these creatures posing as legitimate business owners, who peddle drugs and participate in organised crime. The reality of a vicious cycle of goal/broken relationships and a seedy existence is now not a major influence for Greg Kelly. I'd like to meet this young apprentice Greg Kelly. Can you organise it?"

Alex and Jenny were stunned, nodding only. The Birthmark had surprised them once again. They had no idea what Simon Dang intentioned.

Next morning they arrived in plain clothes (as usual) to Greg Kelly's home near the Cooks River valley.

Greg answered the door putting on his coat. He was on his way out to attend an interview for a job he really didn't want as a car mechanic with a local car dealer.

"Morning. I am Jenny – this is Alex. We are Police Officers looking for Greg Kelly. Would that be you?"

Marie Kelly appeared ay Greg's side. Greg was silent and horrified.

"Come in Officers. I am Marie, Greg's Mum. This is my son, Greg Kelly."

"Thank you."

The two visiting Officers sat in the simple lounge room and took it all in. Clean and comfortable, they were visiting good people. It's obvious to Police Officers. Greg stood nervously nearby as Jenny tried to break the ice.

"We have been part of the investigating team at your former workplace, Greg. Could you tell us a bit about the workplace?"

"I am out of a good job because of your team. Now I have to find another job, actually I have an interview in 30 minutes. Can this talk wait? Or is this another unwanted intervention order?"

Jenny and Alex were used to the tone and stood immediately. Alex handed a card to Greg.

"Call when you can, we understand, our business is not urgent and not part of the investigation. We want to assist you actually."

Greg took the card and stormed out of the house to his interview with the car dealer. Marie Kelly was embarrassed.

"Can I offer tea? Maybe I can fill in some of the gaps. Greg dearly loved that job, you know."

The Officers sat again. They needed information and this was an opportunity.

"Tea would be welcome, thanks Marie."

"He is such a solitary young man and he found real joy and learning at the Rebels Repair Shop. I could see him growing as a person and that's grand for a Mother."

Marie knew she was missing something as the Police officers looked at each other.

"Marie, it was a toxic business being run upstairs in that building. We can't divulge much but your son, Greg is certainly better off out of there. It will be in the news and the people who own that business face prosecution and goal time."

Marie Kelly showed no emotion but was very concerned at this news.

"I have asked Greg to man up and take a disappointment on the chin. He will come around and I will encourage him to call you. Thank you for coming and taking an interest in my son. Greg never spoke about what went on and said only his bosses were treating him well."

"Cheers Marie."

Alex and Jenny reported back their inability to invite young Greg to a 'surf with The Birthmark'.

"Is Greg Kelly a surfer?"

Alex and Jenny laughed together.

"We don't know!"

"OK. We are going to make him a test case to impress on the Commissioner how we can dissuade young people from getting involved with Bikie gangs and their business. What do you think?"

"I have never come across a young man whom I am more certain of with regard to character. He seems to be a very good bike mechanic that loved his work and learning his trade. Our actions have put up a barrier to that and he's not happy with Police types like us. This is predictable."

"Well, you two are trouble on four legs sometimes!.......nahhh only kidding. Please do some research on Greg's profile so I can submit our activity formally to Billy Mason, the Commissioner?"

"We are on it. I am going to keep trying to get him to talk to us. But I need some leverage. Can *we* find him a job maybe?"

Alex was impressed. He knew that would be persuasive to a young man recently unemployed.

"Good idea, Jenny. That would get him onside. Do we have any contacts in the motorcycle repair world?"

The Birthmark said;

"Leave that to me. I have a contact."

The Birthmark made some calls and got a good response from two Dealers who surfed at Maroubra. Next day Jenny put a file in his secure 'in tray' on the veranda of his home as it was afternoon and Simon Dang was sleeping. The profile delivered was thin with detail as Greg Kelly was a young man with a good record.

The interview was necessary to give background and make the opportunity that Simon had in mind accepted.

Simon arrived dripping one morning in the next week after his morning surf to find three individuals on his veranda. The previous night he had put in some solid hours. Simon knew two of them and stuck out his hand to the third young man.

"Greetings. Greg Kelly is it. I am Simon Dang. I am happy to meet you at last."

They shook hands with Simon gently turning over Greg's hand to examine it. Greg Kelly looked at the eyelids of this small man carrying a surfboard (like everybody who meets Simon for the first time). The eyelid birthmarks were distinctive. Greg was nervous but Jenny and Alex had given assurances on the drive over from Greg's home twenty five kilometres away.

"Come in please, all of you. I will get changed quickly. The surf was super this morning."

Jenny and Alex exchanged smiles. Greg looked upbeat at hearing this and silently thought that this Birthmark bloke maybe, an ordinary character, someone you could talk to. Two minutes later Simon reappeared in the lounge room and they all could hear the kettle whistling in the background.

"So Greg, I am going to give you a look at the profile we have on you –it is official but there is nothing to fear. Everything is 'Official' in Police work! We seek to know a few things about your former workplace and in exchange I have exciting news. Have a look and then we will explain. Tea coming up."

Greg perused the documents and noted an email from Harley-Davidson Australia. He skipped past it and the summary of education and activity known. He then waited for the questions and returned to the emails. In his own mind he knew all of them were trying to help. He wanted to co-operate now that his upstairs bosses had gone to Long Bay Goal. That news had shocked him.

"Greg please tell us about how you cracked it for a job with the Rebel Repair Shop?"

Greg told the story of clutch starting a big Harley in the pub car park.

"So you joined a bike club of enthusiasts, then the Rebels found you and offered you an apprenticeship in their repair shop. Is that correct? Were there conditions attached to the job?"

"Yeah. They offered me a job when I had few prospects. And I love motorcycles-fixing them especially. Many riders are decent people. It was a regular apprenticeship from my view and they wanted quality work from Joe and myself in all circumstances."

"No argument. Next I would like to know if you were aware of any the business dealings in that upstairs office area? You need to tell me now of any involvement in their affairs. I believe you are an honest person."

"No. It was a closed shop. I was busy with bikes and unimportant enough not to put two and two together.

They treated me well having said that."

"C'est la vie. Well, read the emails in the file and we will see what interests you. Its compensation for what these 'two wallopers' here have done to you career."

Greg's eyes widened and his 'Adams apple' bobbled up and down while reading. Jenny and Alex were trying to gauge Greg's thoughts. Simon knew they had hit the right process.

"Shit. It can't be true!"

"All verifiable Greg. They will meet you when you are ready."

"Thanks heaps. Harley-Davidson Australia! They have all the best equipped shops. Man, this is seventh heaven. Stoke Avoca! Isn't that what the surfies used to say?"

The Birthmark was delighted with this interaction with Greg Kelly and amused.

"Maybe when Henry Lawson was in short pants in the 1900's. Now we are going to wait till you finalise your personal career path, then with your permission we are to submit this profile and information as a case study for the Police Commissioner. Greg we want to deter young people from joining these bikie gangs."

"I will keep in contact with Alex and Jenny and I hope it's done very soon. Thank you Simon. Wait till I tell Mum. By the way —what did you see in my hand earlier?"

"Potential in spades, my friend."

Chapter 10

T he surf at Maroubra Beach in Sydney's Eastern Suburbs has a typical forecast; The North end works best on a big swell, but it will be crowded and the locals are very talented. A steep, fast wave which can be dumpy. Not one for the faint hearted, and don't expect a long ride unless your confident enough to go out on a big day and mix with the locals. South end of the beach is a touch more mellow, but still an aggressive and talented crowd. Gets shelter from southerly winds and waves are so often a bit more manageable. Best surf in Sydney at Maroubra. Simon Dang, The Birthmark to all his surfie mates, like it that way and tried to get to the beach each morning.

Alex Sutcliffe organised a 'flash mob' of unannounced singers from his Musical Society performers at the big shopping 'town' in Eastgardens. On a regular Saturday morning, Alex had twenty singers assemble one by one in the main square of the shop complex and commence singing. This stopped the crowd of shoppers as the group were good and sang for fifteen minutes. All the kids with their Mothers dropped coins in a hat placed in front of the singers, thinking they were raising money for the Musical Society and their shows.

Alex had other ideas and before the assembled singers could dissolve into the shops he got on bended knee with an engagement ring. He asked his girlfriend Nicole (drawn out sheepishly from the group of singers) to marry him.

Everyone witnessing this was delighted by the event as Nicole held her face crying and totally embarrassed by Alex. However she nodded yes and got him up for a huge hug. Huge applause all round from the onlookers enjoying the surprise treat. Included in the crowd was Jenny Dolan, Alex's Police partner undercover and she had a big smile on her face. Jenny was with her husband, Thomas, for a change and had just informed him this morning that were going to have a baby. Thomas was just coming to terms with this good news and would not Jenny go. He held her hand constantly and escorted her everywhere except to the shower. Jenny knew he was delighted.

Thomas Dolan worried constantly about his wife and her Police duty, often wondering if she will be home at the end of her shift. News of a Policeman being shot in a bank heist in Queensland was more evidence for Thomas' anxiety. It seems a motorcycle cop had driven past whilst the bank robbers were inside, he had stopped and called into the hotline for support, then investigated by moving to the front doors and seeing the armed men rifling through the Teller stations. Drawing his firearm, he identified himself and called a halt to the robbery. He was fired upon and mortally wounded whilst himself wounding two of the three hooded robbers.

The death of that Officer caused Thomas that weekend to think....... "Thank God it wasn't Jenny or Alex."

Being married to a Police Officer, Thomas found was totally different to being married to a regular wife. As they both had commitments, holidaying was difficult and of course he had to accept that the job for Jenny was dangerous. Now she was pregnant, what Thomas wanted was for her to leave the Police. Jenny didn't see it that way as working undercover with Alex and Simon Dang, the Birthmark was a joy for her. They argued about this quite a bit.

Chapter 11

The magnificent reticulated python is one of the most impressive snakes of Southeast Asia. At its greatest size it marginally exceeds 10 metres, which makes this snake one of the longest in the world. This snake occurs throughout S.E.Asia and most islands of the Indo-Malayan archipelago. This snake is an excellent swimmer. In cities, such as Kuala Lumpur and Singapore they are often found in drainage channels of those urban areas.

Oliver Hickey was an Animal Handler of long standing, representative of Taronga Zoo in Sydney. He was currently in Singapore to pick up a reticulated python from the Singapore Zoo. He had spent the early morning at a jungle breakfast with the wildlife and it all brought a smile to his lined face. The Singapore Zoo is set in 69 acres of rainforest and has open concept to better enjoy the wonders of nature, it certainly was working for Oliver Hickey.

"We will complete the paperwork and the transfer to the airport of your python after 09:00. Is this OK with you? Our Office facility does not work Zoo hours."

"Fine with me. The flight to Sydney is late this afternoon. Let's hope my snake passenger sleeps well during the flight."

"Hi Simon. Alex is on his honeymoon and you will have to deal with a pregnant undercover wife for this week at least."

Simon laughed with joy.

"Jenny you are in the pitch of health despite looking like an elephant. You may find it difficult to get near the bench to make tea later but I love working with you."

Jenny covered her smile with her hand.

"I will get right to our business for this morning. Overnight, we have a lost child with a request for help. He is an intellectually compromised young man in the forest on the mid north coast. It is 15 hours in and thelocal Police seek advice. In the past you have asked for a personal item to establish a connection so I have requested same from Northern Area Command. ETA this afternoon. I have details when you are ready.

Next we have an escaped python from the Taronga Park Zoo, described as green and yellow and about five metres long. They want assistance not only how it escaped but where is it now?"

"Call Chuck Ventura, the Pet Detective!"

"I think the character's name was Ace Ventura, Simon."

"I have never been on a lost snake hunt. Any suggestions?"

"The Zoo is quite embarrassed as the reptile house is relatively new and security of the fauna, so to speak, is high on their list of duties. It's a ....here it is, a Malaysian green and yellow python."

"Should be a cinch. Any former escapes?"

Simon was giggling and that set off Jenny.

"No. This snake is a new arrival apparently."

"Obviously didn't like the accommodation and has scarpered."

"It is considered a risk to the public –if someone found it the backyard or hiding in the washing basket."

"Let's get the snake charmers and reptile experts involved and I will concentrate on the lost youth up the coast. Agreed?"

"Agreed. I am putting a profile together currently."

Jenny's phone rang. Simon waited and hoped it was information for their lost young man. Jenny returned and was busily writing down information as Simon's fax machine kicked into life with a few pages printing.

"Simon, I have a problem with my right foot. The sole. Do you mind if I sit and remove my shoes while I summarise the incoming info?"

"I have a better idea. Lay down on the settee over there and I will remove your footwear and examine this problem. Did you know that the Japanese keep track of newborn feet patterns as a means of ID?"

"No. But I will be embarrassed if you massage my feet. I won't let my husband do that!"

"This is as intimate as we can get Jenny."

Simon was laughing as he held Jenny's sockless right foot and gently massaged the sole. He watched Jenny relaxed and closed her eyes.

"Ohhhhhhhhhhhh. That's so good. What causes itchy feet?"

"Jenny, seriously. Itchiness in a pregnant woman at your stage is a symptom of possible bad news. Have you had a blood pressure check lately? When is your next appointment?"

"Keep going please. Sorry –I have forgotten all about our lost boy."

Jenny's phone rang again. She listened and her face showed an expression of delight.

"Oh wonderful news. I will inform the boss. Thanks."

Simon continued his massage therapy, patiently waiting on the 'wonderful news'.

Jenny was giggling with a range of emotions.

"They found him in a washing basket in the laundry. Door locked and he must have crawled through the window. How did I know that! Covered in a sheet and towels overnight and still asleep. Can you 'see' anything from the lines on my soles?"

"Yes, you are pregnant. Is the itching mild or severe? There is a condition called obstetric cholestasis which could lead to drama. Go see your doctor."

"Mild. But can we do the foot massage trick again sometime?"

"Jenny, we have a snake to catch! Please get your mind on Police business."

Jenny's phone rang again. The Police Commissioner, Billy to his friends. Jenny was a favourite.

"Hi Billy, yes Police Avenger Simon Dang is here."

The phone was handed to Simon.

"Yes Sir."

"They found the boy. Alex is back when? I have a situation for you and your team. OK ring me when you find the bloody snake. We have a Terrorist on the doorstep. Tactical Operations Unit have details."

Next morning found the beach soggy from overnight rain and The Birthmark had forgotten his wetsuit. He turned around and found a Café on the way home, bought an expresso and headed home.

Winter was coming.

Alex returned from his honeymoon and glowed with happiness. His only concern was Nicole's (his new wife) serious misgivings about Alex's job. She wasn't asking him to quit but they had had some deep and meaningful discussions during their sailing trip through the South Pacific.

Simon ticked off his list from the previous overnight's work;

"We need to speak to Oliver Hickey at Taronga Zoo."

Alex rang the Zoo and identified himself, he was put through to a very unhappy Oliver Hickey.

"Oliver, this is Alex Sutcliffe. I am a Police Officer wondering how we can help find your snake?"

"Hi Alex. Most concerning for us but this Malaysian species is an escape artist and a long one. He is six metres long and still growing. He is not hungry and searching for food, the bugger just doesn't want to be incarcerated here. He will be in a drain or perhaps a tree. The worry is he may have made it to the harbour down there and they are good swimmers. We may have lost him. The search has been thorough between here and the Ferry Wharf."

"Oliver, is it likely he will be in someone's backyard shed or garden?"

"Possible. We are combing the area but they can move quickly and he was discovered gone early yesterday afternoon."

Simon clucked as the challenge of finding an elusive swimming snake was on the table.

"I know where we start looking. Alex can you and Jenny get a Police launch? We are going on a harbour Cruise and I don't want to miss this one."

Alex and Jenny got cracking, neither had commandeered a Police launch before let alone be on one, but mention of The Birthmark got things happening. They were on the Ferry Wharf at Circular Quay an hour later. Simon with a picnic basket for them all. The 'boatie' Police were amused, especially in a quest to find a snake in the enormous Sydney harbour. However they were all interested in a close up with the legend.

In time they searched Goat Island and moored then on Hen and Chicken Island. Simon had a huge hat on and sat beneath the fruit trees that were in abundance. They all ate lunch and searched some more for a snake. Lo and behold there wrapped around a large leafy lemon tree was the cylindrical shape of a yellow and green snake. Perfectly camouflaged by the dappled sunlight filtering through the lemons and foliage.

Jenny whipped out her phone and called Oliver Hickey at the Zoo. The Water Police grew couldn't stop laughing but the reputation of The Birthmark as a detective grew and grew because of the incident.

Billy Mason, the Police Commissioner shook his head for most of the day after hearing that Simon, the bloody Birthmark had found the missing? Lost snake on an island in Sydney harbour. It was the funniest thing he had heard in years but the implications of setting Simon Dang a detective task were high he would accomplish it.

"Hi Simon. Can we get you out of the Zoo business and shift to a potential Terrorist migrant?"

"Yes Sir. I will contact Tactical Operations and see what can be done. The snake is rescued and fine Sir."

Billy Mason smiled despite his anxiety over a potential Terrorist arrival to NSW.

"Simon, this bloke has applied for a visa. His brother is a known terrorist offender and his sister is in goal in Pakistan for manslaughter. What a family. The details come from Border Security and they rate this guy, Abdul Mohammed Rehman as a danger. Stamped as refused. He's appealing the decision and therefore we need to be prepared as such. Can you review it all and we will talk."

Chapter 12

"OK boss. Do you think that this person will use violence to express his views here in Sydney? I would have thought that any chance of that would deny him a visa."

"Exactly. Talk soon my friend."

Simon reviewed the application and made some notes about reducing the lure of violent extremist ideologies and the likelihood of reducing counter-terrorism efforts by excluding this person. He filed a report to the Department of Foreign Affairs and Trade as such and forgot about it. Simon was convinced that Australia does not need these hateful people. Weeks later the Australian Government Minister for Foreign Affairs rang Simon.

"Hi Simon. This is Herbert Merle, we have not met but I have your profile and reputation in hand. Do you have a minute to talk about this visa for an individual, let me see Abdul Mohammed Rahmen?"

"Of course Minister."

"Grand. I find this application repulsive personally but I would like to hear your opinion."

"Sir, thank you for the call. I would firstly confirm my support for the denial of this visa application. Second I would describe my country as the best place to live in this world and perhaps understand this man trying to migrate. I am conscious that he has family here and of course we now have eyes on these individuals, that I find to be progress. Lastly, I would say that the Counter Terrorism Team have done their job. Super, in fact. They deserve your support, Sir."

"Thanks Simon. I concur and I'm glad you are on our team as I am becoming aware of you contribution."

"Goodbye Minister."

Simon looked at the clock. It was 03:00hrs, his working time but a Minister of the Federal Government up at this hour? Unbelievable.

Simon returned to his research for Billy Mason. That man was a good hearted devil. Simon had had conversations with the Police Commissioner that were definitely not for publication in recent times.

"Simon, this is the truth. The public perception is that senior police are more concerned about progressing internal issues like gender-balanced promotion than they are about protecting our public from criminals and would be terrorists. How do you figure that?"

"Sir. We have to realise there is no perfect solution. Your Police Force people are set up for failure, as human beings will always stuff up and leave a mess. We have at best, temporary periods of calm."

Simon waited. Billy Mason got up and shook Simon on the shoulder, then leaving without comment.

Boris, the Dobermann, Lucky Lermentov's former companion animal made the Police newsletter with photos;

'Reformed Boris has graduated from the Dog Squad Training Facility and on his first outing chased down a burglar in a unit complex at

Riverwood. The suspect was arrested during a search of the premises. The suspect came quietly reported the Dog handler Constable Harrison. Boris apparently frightened the daylights out of the alleged burglar.'

"Well done, Boris."

Jenny was amused and delighted. Alex, also a dog lover, was pleased Boris had adapted to the training.

"Good news story."

Simon heard the discussion whilst he was using a Police big-data analytical tool to identify patterns of crime and predicting future crime through mapping of a high risk area in the city. Simon was attempting to predict certain types of crime. It will give frontline Police a 'heads up' to conduct patrols more effectively.

Also new on the horizon was the Police body-worn cameras will be programmable to use facial recognition software. Police on foot patrols would be able to apprehend any person for whom a national or international arrest warrant has been issued. Simon liked the sound of that.

"Jenny, Alex. I am going to be missing the next two days. Red Dust are sending me two ten year olds from the Northern Territory to learn how to surf and enjoy the big smoke."

"Simon. What is Red Dust, you forget we are just city coppers."

"Red Dust is an organisation encouraging Indigenous youth to learn more about health, enrich their lives and strengthen their future through a mentoring system. Give the kids a positive role model in sport, art, music and dance. I don't qualify for any of those things but Billy Mason our boss has asked me to take time out and teach Arthur and Jeanette how to surf. These kids will travel a long way to a freak show like me but Billy insists that I participate."

"Can we help too? I mean Alex ....would you be willing?"

"Absolutely. Sounds like fun. Can the work wait?"

Simon was stunned.

"OK, we will all have two days off. If this works for the Red Dust organisation, we may well be digging ourselves into an ongoing commitment."

"Can't wait. This stuff is why I am a Police Officer. Simon, by the way I can't surf either."

Alex looked sheepish.

"You will have to teach us all!"

Next day they waited on the veranda of Simon's home in the early morning. The sun was already up and with a warm gentle breeze it looked like a good weather day. Soon a station wagon arrived with an adult male and two Indigenous students in their board shorts and T shirts. Each had a back pack and the driver came up the path with a huge smile on his face. Unlike Simon who was not a social type and apprehensive.

"Greetings. I am John. Please meet Jeanette and Arthur."

The kids were giggling with excitement and looking at the three of them and overawed by all the traffic and noise. They noticed Simon's eyelids but politely refused to ask questions. Good kids.

"Hiya."

They both shouted and shook hands with Simon, Alex and Jenny.

"Come in please."

Simon was a good host and encouraged the two kids to try all the seats and lounges. John asked.

"Simon, there are three of you. Have I been misinformed?"

"Yes and No. These two Police Officers work with me and if you can keep a secret, they work undercover.

But on hearing of our boss's directive to teach surfing they want to assist and broaden the terms of reference in the next two days. In other words they want to spoil Jeanette and Arthur so that they go home to their mates and brag. Simple."

John was delighted as he had been apprehensive about this excursion. NSW Police are unusual sponsors.

"Great. Is there anything you need from me, otherwise I will see you in 48 hours."

"See ya. It will be OK."

They shook hands again. John said goodbye to the kids who were channel surfing already on Simon's TV.

"OK. Let's hit the beach!"

Both the kids jumped up with excitement and picked up their back packs. Climbing over each other.

"Ready, Simon."

Jenny and Alex had already requisitioned a big van for two days. Billy Mason's name opens a lot of doors. They sat the kids in the back seats with all the boards and gear and checked their seatbelts.

"Is this a real Police car?"

"Sure is, Arthur."

Alex turned on the flashing lights and the siren on the way to Maroubra Beach. The kids both were over the moon screaming with delight and watched transfixed as the traffic got out of the way for two Indigenous surfer students and three very amused adults on the way to the beach. They arrived more quietly and carefully manoeuvred the kids safely after parking.

Lucky the sea was sparkling and the wonder was in their eyes. The three adults stood back and watched Arthur and Jeanette's faces as they surveyed Maroubra Beach from the huge Surf Club near the southern end.

"We can both swim. We learned in the pool. Jeanette is the champ."

Jeanette, obviously the quiet one looked at the surf and trembled. Simon had missed nothing.

"Today we walk up and down barefoot, we get wet and we try to stand up on the boards with a small wave. All in shallow water as this is the Pacific Ocean and if you swim out you might end up in New Zealand."

The kids nodded only. Not one of the adults had a clue how much they had taken in. It didn't matter.

Jenny took Jeanette's hand and they walked up and down absorbing, with the others, the smells and the waves with their crashing sounds. For Arthur and Jeanette it was magic. Arthur held tight to Simon's handas he trembled with delight. As the water swirled around their feet, Arthur asked;

"Simon, the water is cold –how can we swim. We are from hot country!"

"You can keep your T-shirt on, no problem. This ocean water is salty but very clean. You will feel refreshed in no time."

"What's refreshed?"

Jeanette had been listening.

"It means good feeling, Arthur."

"OK. Are you ready to swim first and feel the power of the sea? C'mon!"

The two kids stood in the water hand in hand with the three adults and felt the surge of the water breaking in front of them and then the tug of the water going back out. Jeanette was the first to dive into the broken wave and came up with a huge smile on her wet face. Arthur saw all this and was next but got a mouthful of sea water and was temporarily scared. Alex looked after him and showed him how to dive in the shallow water safely. An hour later they were learning how to catch a small wave and keep their small bodies rigid to ride the wave into the beach. It was tons of fun and exhausting.

Sitting on the beach with towels around them and shivering numb from the cold, each adult took turns to hug them and try to keep them warm. It was in their eyes though that these two kids were digesting this new and tiring experience. Hungry Arthur was first;

"Simon, can you ask these Police officers to find us some tucker?"

The three adults fell about laughing and on seeing this the kids did too.

"We will go to Maccas on the way home soon. You need to tell us when you have had enough. We will be back here tomorrow."

"Can we put the siren on when we drive to Maccas?"

"No. That's for emergencies only. When we get home we have a raft of activities planned like going to the movies in the city and lots of healthy eating. John will have a fit when he finds out we went to MacDonalds!"

The kids just grinned, they were happy. They set about building sand castles and Jenny spent quite a while bringing water up to their sand castles to show them how to consolidate them. The morning sun was getting too much for Simon so they left the beach and headed off to eat. That done, both kids were tired and fell asleep in the car on the way home. The three adults then took turns to supervise them as they prepared some computer games before lunch. Both these kids had great imagination and the educational computer games they took to very quickly. That early evening they took the kids to the Sydney Cricket Ground for an AFL match. This was a highlight for them both as they both played Aussie Rules football at home in the Northern Territory of Australia. Alex took them down to the fence after the game as the players were heading off the field and one of the Sydney Swans champions, Lance Franklin saw the two Indigenous kids there with Alex and came over to say hello and shake their hands. It was a joy for them both and Alex thanked Lance 'Buddy' Franklin profusely. Buddy signed their T shirts and when they got back to Simon and Jenny they were ecstatic.

"Can we take our T-shirts off and put them in our bags, Simon?"

"No. Buddy would want you to wear them proudly as Indigenous people do, after all he is a great role model, don't you think?"

They kept their T shirts on and revelled in the SCG singing the Swans winning song after they won. Alex and Jenny headed off home and Simon was happy that the first day had gone so well. Simon took the kids home to vegetable soup and toast with some fruit to finish off. They played card games before both of the kids needed some sleep. It had been a big day.

Next day they did a harbour cruise and visited Oliver Hickey in the Reptile House of the Zoo. They checked on the escaping python from Malaysia who was curled up sleeping. The noise and smells were exotic to them and they enjoyed the seal show and feeding the

Giraffes. Both Arthur and Jeanette imitated the calls of the wild animals during the day with astonishing accuracy.

They got home to Simon's late afternoon exhausted but wanting to "go for a surf." This was a twilight swim where both Jeanette and Arthur were photographed by Jenny, dripping wet on the beach. Both kids managed to stand on the Malibu boards beaming at Jenny and Alex. Simon was laughing waist deep in the break. Of course, the kids insisted on repeating the surfing till it grew dark. Once home Jenny and Alex departed happy and promised to see the kids before John turned up to take them to the airport.

Overnight, Jenny printed a series of photographs demonstrating the kids surfing and laughing on the Boards. She placed them in plastic envelopes to protect them and she hoped they would show them to their friends when they got home. The goodbyes next morning were tough as the kids wanted to stayand they had formed a bond with the three adults. Simon assured them they would stay in contact through John and the organisation Red Dust.

"Thanks heaps. Can we come back?"

Jeanette was no longer the shy one. Arthur smiled at the good idea. Alex said;

"We would be glad to see you anytime, so we don't have to work. It has been fun."

They all shook hands as John appeared on the verandah. Simon smiling;

"When you are next in Sydney, come and see me. Here is a card for each of you. We'll catch a few waves."

The kids pocketed the cards as if it was precious to them.

"Thanks for the photos. We had a great time. See ya."

Simon made tea as they assessed the time spent on the kids to their extensive workload.

"We should be all right. Billy will be patient as we catch up. First duty is to research the potential migration with the Terrorist family."

"Simon. I am on Maternity leave next week. I am happy to take on the research so I can be in one place, that is the Office. I am finding a bit hard to get about. Learning to surf at 33/40 weeks is tough"

"OK. Alex will have to pull the load whilst we find another assistant to do your tasks. Any recommendations?"

Alex hoped for a good partner like Jenny. He was forthright.

"Jenny, could we ask Isabella Cassali from Parramatta headquarters. Billy Mason knows her work and as he will have to approve the appointment, we could quicken the process."

"I like Bella, but she's a control freak. A hot tempered Italian. She is organised, but will take over."

"Not another boss!"

Simon shook his head;

"Let's talk to her all together. Can you set it up, then I can talk to Billy Mason. He may have an opinion that we might have to accede to?"

"Done."

The interview meeting proceeded once Billy Mason, Police commissioner gave the go ahead. It was the daybefore Jenny's departure.

"Isabella or is it Bella. I am Simon Dang. Welcome."

"I am Isabella Cassali, Bella is fine and thank you. Jenny has given some insight into her role here. The undercover bit I have first-hand knowledge of from my time a few years ago."

"There is a lot of routine Police research and preparation of information in this job. Alex can show you the ropes but I am more interested in your ambitions. This role is not for everybody. Some days you will be dizzy with the workload."

"I am prepared to work hard. Ambitions for me lay with making a contribution. I like the Police and this role holds interest for me. That summarises my response."

"Good. May I suggest a period of dual evaluation. You evaluate what is being asked of you and I will evaluate your work. Agreed?"

"Agreed."

"Alex or Jenny. Comment please."

Alex liked the look of Bella and he was trusting of Jenny's support.

"Let's give the dear old thing a chance."

Bella went pink but smiled. Jenny was horrified but used to Alex's sense of humour. Simon thought perhaps it was a test of Bella's sense of humour. Simon stood smiling;

"See you all tomorrow as the team begins a new phase."

Bella punched Alex in the upper arm behind Simon's back. Alex looked hurt and surprised.

"Bastard."

She hissed, but was amused.

"Jenny, we have a present for you. Please have a healthy child and enjoy being a Mother. The world needs motherhood."

"Thanks. You are kind as usual."

Jenny opened up a beautiful blanket that was so soft and beautifully well crafted.

"It is gorgeous! Wonderful. I am looking forward to being a Mother. Thank you so much."

Chapter 13

John, at Red Rust responded to Simon's minor forty eight hours of diversion from work with Jeanette and Arthur and informed the Police Commissioner that Simon's Surf school was a raging success. Red Dust have a line-up of Indigenous young Australians wishing to come to Maroubra. Simon, two days later, answered the phone one early morning getting ready to hit the beach. He was impatient to have some recreation and reluctantly answered the phone. The familiar voice of the boss quelled his impatience and increased his concentration.

"Simon, my friend, we are going to have to increase your remuneration so that you can accommodate these many young Aussies who want to camp in Maroubra!"

"Thank you, Sir. Arthur and Jeanette were wonderful kids. I've been thinking that with your permission we could send a Police bus up there and grab a bunch of them all at once. I have lined up the Surf School at Maroubra and they can handle twenty at once for a nominal fee. We just have to devise a program around the beach and I know, Sir, you are on a winner."

"I knew this call was going to cost me money. Let me get our experts on the case. It is exciting though for us as coppers in NSW to help these NT kids. Warms my heart among all the normal news."

"I agree, Sir. Your Indigenous youth program will bring a lot of credit to NSW Police."

"True. But I have to find the funds, Simon. Leave it with me, now I have the bit between me teeth. Let me see if I can bounce some of these accountant types out of their comfort zone."

Simon hung up and went surfing. Happy with his small contribution. His thoughts now moved to the 'new girl' starting with his fractured team today. He wished for success as he watched the surf and waxed his board. Simon didn't require anyone but someone who could work diligently and had a sense of humour.

In the days to come Bella did her best to fit right in and Simon admired her attitude. As per his routinehe examined her personal records to gauge her strengths and weaknesses. Simon had to know with whomhe was working. He found in Isabella Cassali a good Cop, perhaps an exceptionally determined woman. He would test her as he had Jenny and Alex earlier and watch for the pattern of activity. Bella either had the substance or not. That time came quickly with Alex visiting his sick Mother on the North Coast of NSW.

Bella was on her own.

"Simon, I have tried to answer all your 23 pages of questions on this so called Terrorist bloke wanting to migrate but I'm struggling to understand the minute detail you require. In Australian Law consorting with criminals is an offence. First question then, how can that influence an application for a visa if it is a family member that's an offender and the migrant applicant is clean. How then can Border Security reject the application. It's not logical......my sister is a bitch, therefore I am as well?"

"Understand your reserve, but here we are in a legal minefield. The detail is very important to a final conclusion from this Office. They look for an independent view from us, therefore we must have 23 pages of detail to support that view. I am challenged constantly."

"OK. I will ask no more of these type of questions. I am finished with the profile thankfully."

"Would you allow this person to migrate to Australia?"

"No. My gut feeling he is a cleanskin recruiter and will inflame and spread the hatred they believe in."

"I agree. Let's turn our attention to the drones now available to Police. Have you read the dossier?"

"Yes. Fascinating. Finding troublemakers at the football stadium with a drone –I like it. I have been onduty at the Sydney Football stadium trying to extract a drunk or obnoxious person. It is not easy even to find them and get them out of there. The deterrent element for people to behave is a positive I believe."

"Well done. Bella how is your motivation for this job going?"

"I am definitely stimulated. The tempo is first class, but I am getting fat doing all this research! Simon, I am sitting on my arse too much. Do you mind if I exercise through the day?"

"Not only do I not mind, I insist that you take an hour out of every day here to exercise."

Simon laughed and looked at Bella without looking so to speak. Bella eyeballed OK to him. Actually since Bella had turned up with the Team, Simon had become aware of perfume smells, body postures and attire that Bella brought to the workplace which he had never been aware of previously. Jenny was always private as she was married and Simon only noticed her femininity. With Bella it was the full capsule. Bella was a single woman and apparently a divorcee. Even though that had never been discussed.

As Simon was nocturnal, it presented a problem for someone like Bella. She was used to using her influence. Simon had given her time each morning to get the work underway, then the bugger would go off to sleep. Bella had no one to bounce off as Alex was away. It was stimulating work and she tried her best but needed someone to influence, such was her nature. Simon solved the problem when Boris, the Dobermann was injured during a Police operation. He was fixed up by the Vet, but no longer could work as a Police dog such were his injuries. Simon put his hand up to take Boris as a pet and there started a beautiful friendship.

Boris lapped up the constant attention. Simon spoiled Boris. Simon and Boris became inseparable except at the beach while Simon surfed. Simon found the situation amusing as the local Council Inspectors tried to give him a $300 fine for having a dog on the beach. Boris watched on but his ability to survey the situation was limited. Simon's Federal Police Minder took the Council Inspector aside and explained that the dog would remain on this beach. The Council Inspector fumed;

"Here's the ticket, no dogs allowed on Maroubra beach. Get your dog off the beach quick smart of I will get the Dog Catcher to take the beast to the Pound!"

"I have shown you my badge and now I am going to rip up your ticket as you are not listening."

"Whose bloody dog is it anyway?"

"Good day."

"I am going to submit the ticket and your version of this conversation."

No one tried again to give Simon a ticket for Boris who watched his every move.

The Minder had walked away. Boris woofed in support and probably because Simon came up the beach waving. Boris was a very good companion animal despite his past. It was just that Bella was too much for him. Boris slept on the couch most days. Just so long as no one threatened Simon. Boris was unable to accept much patting from Bella, who avoided the Dobermann and the couch after a few growling incidents.

Bella did comment, ignorant of Boris's past.

"Simon, that dog is a killer."

"You better believe it."

As the days unfolded Bella grew in confidence and appreciation of her new role. Simon no longer considered her the 'new girl' and piled on the administrative work so that when Alex returned, there was a distinct change (for the better) in collaboration between the three. Alex noticed a re hash of their Office nearby which demonstrated Bella's organisational skills and a ruthless efficiency was prominent in the caseload. Simon had a word to Alex the first morning of his return.

"Let her change whatever she wants in the Office. Her work is daily improving and we are refining our priority system so we can attend to those phone calls for help, especially Canberra, when they arrive. Bella is very good on the phone and is now protecting me."

Simon was grinning.

"I have Minders everywhere!"

Alex was interested and really didn't care about the office. The work was paramount.

"I can work with her. She's good company as well. By the way -any news from Jenny?"

"No."

Chapter 14

At that moment, Jenny was perspiring after more than a few hours in the Coast Hospital Delivery Suite, her hand held by a gowned Thomas who was also perspiring and wanting this birth over and done. Thomas saw the head appear and a few minutes later their daughter Emily lay in her Mother's arms. Whew.

"Alex, can you help me with Boris. He growls when I go near him."

"It's the canine sense of smell, I think. It is estimated at about fifty times a humans in sensitivity. I suggest a change perfume brand? Give it a try or wear nothing one day."

"Does it annoy you, my odour?"

"Truthfully no. A feminine odour as you put it is a positive with me- but I am not Boris. Bella, the truth forme is bad breath puts me in a spin. That is not an issue here."

"OK. I will not wear any over the weekend. Monday, I will take the beast for a walk if you will answerthe phone during that time."

"Of course. If it doesn't work I will organise a 'Boris the Beast' T-shirt for you."

Bella laughed hard at that. Alex had never heard her laugh so much. Simon was correct, Bella was indeed relaxing and coming to the party as it were. Monday arrived and Alex had Boris's lead in his hand. He checked out by smelling Bella's submitted neck much to her amusement and handed over the lead. Alex had brought Boris over to their Office so that they wouldn't wake Simon after the morning briefing.

"See you soon."

Both returned thirty minutes later tired as Bella had decided to run Boris in the park with a frisbee. Boris went straight to the bowl of water.

"He loves me now! My goodness he has some energy for an older dog. Watch this."

Bella went over to Boris, interrupted his drinking by holding out her hand, Boris licked her hand wet andreturned to his drinking. Boris was then content to find a comfortable spot on his couch and rest.

"Think it was the perfume, you were correct."

Alex waited for Bella to recover and then went through the briefing material. It was all national stuff today from Canberra. Preparation in spades for them both then Simon to provide opinion on a variety of issues.

The office phone rang.

"Bella here."

"Billy Mason, Bella -how is it all going."

"Hi Boss. I have made friends with Boris. Real progress as he detested my perfume it seems. The work is great, I am learning every day. For example, I have three tasks for Canberra today and I'm nearly finished with the preparation for Simon. So I will have time to work on the monthly verbal in your office."

"Glad to hear it all. Please don't hesitate. In fact, I would like you to give this month's report in my Office when you are ready. Tell Simon that I am snooping."

"Yes, Sir. The stats we are keeping are improving and I have tried to improve efficiency with the demands on this office."

"Jenny Dolan has had a girl. My spies at the hospital tell me Mother and child are well."

"Great news, Boss. I will inform the team. See you next week in Parramatta."

"Come to the city. Lunch, I will get Shirley to book you in. Au revoir."

"Thank you, Sir."

The Team, except Boris the Dobermann, turned up with flowers, toys and chocolates for Jenny and her family. They didn't stay long and the happy visitors found deliriously happy parents wanting to take their Emily home. Bella became 'clucky' on the way back to their office. Simon with the obligatory sun hat asked;

"How soon can we catch up to formulate the verbal monthly report for Billy Mason?"

"I've written down some points for your review, after all he wants to hear your opinions. This month I am just the messenger."

"That's progress I reckon. I will call by now or can you email me and I will pick it up on the phone."

Bella did so rapidly whilst Simon stood admiring her efficiency and her stockinged legs for the hospital visit. This woman knows how to power dress he thought. Simon looked down at his dungarees and polo shirt -clean but crumpled. Simon's phone made a trumpet sound as the email notes arrived.

"Thanks Bella. I'm trying to keep up with your efficient process."

"Now Simon I have some ideas to filter the tasks assigned to you. Presently we answer the phone, respond to email / fax or instructions from the boss. We have to capture all requests so that your workload can be examined and your personal priority system can easily be executed. Are you an advocate for change to improve our data analysis, hit rate and records?"

"Bella, you have lost me. Let's go to my place and discuss this 'filtering of tasks'"

"Alex, are you good with this, I won't be long."

"OK. I am going for lunch. Anyone want something from the shops?"

"No thanks."

Simon and Bella were dropped off and Alex disappeared. Boris wagged his tail at both of them and they found him some food while Simon made the inevitable tea, yawning.

"I am going to bed after this."

Simon missed the table, tripped over Boris and threw tea in all directions as he fell banging his head slightly on the floor. Bella copped most of the tea on her skirt, then noticed how groggy Simon was sounding. She went into First -Aid mode and got a pillow off Boris's couch, Boris had scarpered out to the back room during the melee where the surfboard and washing machine was. Bella knelt down besides Simon;

"Simon, you have banged your head. Where is your first aid box/cabinet?"

"Kitchen."

"Wait a second. I'll get it."

Simon was concussed but not bleeding and his breathing and pulse were strong. Boris came back and licked his face.

"Please Bella."

Bella returned to the scene and started to laugh. Covering her mouth what she saw was ridiculous.

"Simon that's the dog! Not me."

Bella thought this hysterical and sat on the floor, exploding with laughter. Boris wagged his tail some more and jumped all over a recovering Simon. Then Bella noticed her tea stained skirt and went back into the kitchen to wipe it down. She took off her shoes and removed her skirt, hidden away as she was in there.

She cleaned up the tea stain but it would need a wash. Simon guessed what she was doing out of sight.

"The washing machine is there if you want to wash it now. I will find you some jeans."

Simon Dang was now up and about, but too soon. He collapsed on the couch and Bella came running back in.

"What are you doing? Stay there please."

"Nice legs, Bella."

Bella went red in the face as she realised her stockings only legs. Then she felt the pressure of a palm up the back of her leg as she leaned over checking Simon again. Bella whispered to him;

"What are you doing with that hand, Simon?"

"I am feeling delirious. You may have to escort me to my bed. Over that way."

Bella, very dubious, helped Simon up and to his very tidy bedroom -that was a surprise. She eased him down onto the bed and tried to take his shoes off. Simon grabbed Bella and they spent the afternoon in bed together. Simon found Bella a willing participant, if the truth be known she had been angling for this particular outcome for some months.

As the sun went down, conversation was deep and meaningful. Simon felt mightily relieved mentally, he was a cerebral creature. The afternoon, of course, had been more than he could hope for in a physical sense. But a sense of calm overwhelmed him and prompted some 'opening up of his thinking'.

"I'm tired of being alone."

Bella waited. She was exhilarated by the encounter with this rare man, he had a perception of the things that must be done to satisfy a woman. Boy did it work for her! She covered herself patiently.

"Simon this has been more for me than companionship."

"Understand please that I don't normally come on to those on the team. I am isolated is what I'm trying to say. Boris excluded -and our conversations are one sided. You have broken down my normal reserve. This happens infrequently. The stats as they say are skinny."

"Please don't think that I throw these occasions around. You are my third partner, including my ex."

"Bella, I am not proposing marriage but I would like to see you very often. This is going to ruin our work for sure. I know one thing, you can't have both. Therefore, if you are interested in me as I am hoping, then we face a decision."

"I would like to keep my private life just that way, Simon. I am content to return to Headquarters and preserve my interest in you to myself. Know that I have enjoyed this workload so much. Now here we are."

"That will work for me as the communication lines will remain between us and my 'social' life."

"You sleep each day and work every night from my observation. What social life are you hiding?"

"I can be social when I'm warmed up-like now. Lets have a beer and celebrate. Are you a drinker, Bella?"

"You bet. What brews does the solitary man have?"

"How about a Great Northern?"

They showered and sat with Boris (he on the couch they on the floor). Beers in hand. Both glowed with happiness while Boris looked from one to the other in confusion. He put his head down and closed his eyes.

"Simon, here's to the antidote for melancholy, cheers."

They clinked glasses. Bella looked at her glass. It looked and felt like Waterford crystal. Impressive.

"Is the antidote beer or sex?..........Do you have a viewpoint on fate?"

"Both. Only your fate if you go out in a big swell to surf and you can't handle it."

"As a 'regular' human being I also have a question about your clairvoyant ability. I am a witness to the predictive ability and mathematical evaluation of facts but you have another ace up your sleeve don't you?"

"I was a star at the local fete. They provided me with a tent, a gypsy outfit and I made a fortune (sic) for the school. I also was considered a freak because of my eyelids. Do you think I'm a freak?"

"Certainly not. More gifted and talented. Is it about contact? Basically what works for you?"

"Yes, in some instances. Lost people can be discovered if there is a tangible personal item to concentrateon as this gives insight but it's hard to explain. But perhaps an example; I was at a conference a year or two ago. Whilst waiting for a session to commence I walked into a room full of attendees and knew straight away who to avoid any contact with in that room."

"Wow - that's intangible."

"Correct. Another beer? I have decided to have this night off. I think our team is on top of things, agreed?"

"Agreed. Can I stay with you?"

"Absolutely. I haven't enjoyed a day like this in living memory."

"One last question, Sir. They have created a legend in our Police force saying you have a 'mega mind'. Sir,

can you confirm or deny these allegations?"

Bella was laughing. She pretended to be taking a statement. Simon smirked.

"I was hopeless at school in many subjects. English – William bloody Shakespeare! I don't get it. So Madam I refute your flimsy allegation."

The conversation ended with kisses.

Bella transferred back to Police headquarters forthwith. This was the end of the former team and Alex and Simon soldiered on by themselves. The benefits for Simon far outweighed the workload problems. He maintained his private life and Bella helped him do it. Alex for his part remained silent but he did wonderto himself what had happened.

Opportunities can surprise you. Simon was approached in a formal manner from the United States Embassy in Canberra. His profile and success rate outstripped their internal statistics and they wanted to know why. Basically all Governments and Police agencies in the world face similar issues. However the USA is a world Policeman informally with their resources and military might. The USA Ambassador himself signed the letter of prospective collaboration. The Birthmark had hit the big time!

Simon Dang forwarded the letter to Billy Mason and the Federal Government for evaluation as this was not decision for himself alone given the international ramifications. Simon unknowingly had caused a major discussion. The Feds were supportive up to a point as was NSW Police Commissioner Billy Mason, now a friend for Simon. The Birthmark was 'their' asset after all.

Details were forthcoming from the USA. There would be a period of consultation for Simon on an overnight basis. This suited Simon as he was working anyway while the rest of the country slept. Facilities and procedure for a Conference call after security clearance was formulated. Simon estimated he would need two more Police staff to contend with the workload. Unprecedented. Billy Mason had other ideas.

"Simon we can tap into the largest crime fighting resources in the world with you as our conduit. InterPol will be next to line up for your services!"

Sadness descended on Simon, his life had become very complicated. Time to progress his personal life was in danger. There was only so much that one individual could manage. He sought advice from Billy Mason.

"Sir, I want to take some leave. Would you agree to it?"

"Simon I have been waiting for you to snap under the workload currently. Now with the Yanks knocking on the door, 'our' precious resource -that would be you, I think, needs some R&R. Tell you what, take that girl of yours away and leave the rest to me."

Billy Mason saw the look of horror come over Simon's face.

"Don't worry, your secret is safe with me."

The Birthmark was relieved to hear that as he had been very careful not to expose Bella, now returned to her former role at Police headquarters, as his partner. It would compromise her position.

"Thanks. Will you respond to the American request when it comes? I am happy to help as you know."

"When you get back you and I will have a deep and meaningful. This request has gone to the highest level here in Australia. Apparently the PM is due to visit the US formally very soon. We have to wait on their direction but I feel that our guys will agree to the collaboration and then I must staff this properly so we can gain something from it. Bon voyage. I do not want to see you for three weeks."

Simon texted Bella.......'*pack your bikini, we have been told to take a holiday by the boss.*'

Simon asked Alex to come down from the office up the road.

"Alex, can you look after Boris for a couple of weeks. If not the Dog squad will accommodate him. I have been ordered to take some leave. Can you hold the fort?"

"OK. About time you did take some leave. Will you be contactable at all?'

"Yes I will check in but infrequently. The boss is looking after matters and he will take your call at any time."

"OK. Boris and I will see you then."

Simon's phoned played a tune that sounded like 'Blue Hawaii'. He smiled and let Alex out of the house.

Closing the door he looked at the phone.

'Yippee. When......?'

'Now if you want.'

'See you in an hour and a half.'

"Hi Surfing Simon."

Bella appeared on the veranda to enter the house with a bag.

"Hiya. How did you know we are going to Hawaii?"

"Where else would a surfer go but the North Shore of Kona..isn't it?"

"OK with you? By the way, the boss is aware of our relationship. The Minders on watch must have informed on us. I just hope it doesn't compromise your job."

"There are other jobs. Worry not, sweetie. Have you booked anything yet?"

"No. Can you fix it?"

"OK. I'm excited."

They flew overnight and arrived in Hawaii after a good sleep. Bella proved she could sleep anywhere on that flight over the Pacific Ocean.

The American proposal came through to Billy Mason via Foreign Affairs. It was brief and specific.

'Please provide opinion on the Middle East. Include Australian Policy and detail as you see fit'.

"Shit."

Billy Mason wondered how his friend The Birthmark could digest that curly subject and advance any nations viewpoint.

Meanwhile Bella and Simon lazed in the shade of a beach house far away from the tourists. They wondered about lunch and reviewed the surfing conditions. Bella was on her fifth magazine for the day. Simon snoozed.

On landing in Hawaii a week ago, the US Customs Passport Control flagged Simon Dang as a person of interest. He was swiftly moved to an interview room. In fact, the two Customs guys read with interest what their computer profile contained. They simply wanted to meet Simon to offer assistance. He was warmly welcomed. One of them immediately went outside to retrieve a nervous Bella. Then it was all smiles and 'welcome to our country'. The Customs leader came in and offered the pair a car for their stay. Simon moved his glasses up his forehead but refused.

"I'm grateful but we would like to keep a low profile. So, could you tell your Minders to stay out of sight?

I am willing to provide an itinerary so we have peace and quiet. You know catch a few waves."

"OK Simon. You and Bella have a fine time, our Government tags you as a VIP. We will be in the background only. That's a guarantee!"

"Thanks. Can we go now?"

"Of course. Enjoy."

The three Customs men discussed Simon's eyelids for a considerable time. None of them had seen a dossier resembling Simon's on the computer before. Fascinating.

Simon surfed Waimea Bay on a quiet day and loved the vibe of the Hawaiian Surfers. They made friends with quite a few just from a conversation on the beach. Australian's were welcome, but too soon it was time to return home and work. The holiday was welcome and their new friends promised to visit and stay in Maroubra when they got to Sydney.

Billy Mason two weeks later had Simon in his office in boardies and T shirt. Simon gave Billy a beer glass from a bar in Hawaii. Billy Mason was forthright;

"Simon, are you giving me a stolen glass? Anyway we have had a bit of a shit storm while you've been on leave. If you are ready, I will fill you in and see if we can navigate our way through these issues."

"I'm listening, Sir."

"The Yanks seem to thrive of drama, its wearing thin with me I can tell you. For example, they want anopinion -forecast more like it on the recent Middle East bombings in Saudi Arabia. The explosive mix of oilprices, people who hate each other and religious extremism."

"Well, that's straight to the nub of all the finger pointing."

"You bet. Trying to sort that lot out will require the wisdom of a Solomon. The balls in your court, Simon."

"Can I have ten minutes, Sir, before responding?"

Billy Mason laughed like a lunatic.

"I'm glad you are back, son."

Simon went home to think before this evening's broadcast from Washington. He did not have strong views on a national level currently –trouble was a constant, more like a viewpoint in historical facts and what could be done to eliminate threats so that all peoples in the Middle East region could get on with their lives.

Simon announced a five year plan with a charter through the United Nations in New York. The Americans listened with amazement at Simon's predictive forecast backed up by mathematical formula. The concept of a Middle East Union to bind the common requirements of all nations in that region was novel. Money and business he spoke for twenty minutes on and he finalised his opinion statement with reasoning on the conservatism endemic in Middle Eastern nations. There was silence at the Washington end, then.

"Thank you, Simon. We have a lot to work on from this recording. Our team has been instructed from the highest level here to find some solutions. You have provided much to work on so quickly. We will be in touch so perhaps you could elaborate. Our CIA guys are nodding in agreement. Thanks again, you will hear from us soon. Good night."

Weeks later Simon was on the phone to the Prime Minister's office in Canberra when the PM came on.

"Good evening, Simon Dang. During my visit to the Oval Office the President wanted to convince me to send you over to the US to work on foreign policy. I told him that was unlikely as there is no surf in Washington. He laughed at that. But a serious offer is on the table. I leave it to you. Thanks again for your priceless contribution to our nation. Keep up the good work. See ya."

Simon looked at his phone in shock. That the unconventional President of the US knew about him was humbling. Simon went to bed.

Chapter 15

Next day there was a confronting case splashed across the news which greatly disturbed Simon Dang. The background was sketchy but the details of the case were horrific. He looked into the file through official channels. What Simon found was a nightmare and he could not believe the extent of some of it. He spoke to Bella at breakfast and she confirmed the information. They discussed statistics and some more facts of what Police have to deal with domestic violence with the frightening waste associated. Simon read some more to piece this event together;

Benton Hull drained his schooner glass and approached the bar. It had been a long hot day pouring concrete and his needs were considerable as he fished out the money for another beer. As he surveyed the bar to his left, waiting for his drink he saw out of the corner of his eye, Olivia Hendersen. His attractive missus opened the Saloon bar door and look into the cool interior.

Too late for Benton Hull to hide, duck and weave. Benton steeled himself for the inevitable confrontation.

Other patrons at the bar recognised there was trouble coming by the smouldering, determined look of the well-dressed woman who had just entered.

Benton grimaced as he returned to his seat, he tried to ignore Olivia's approach. She arrived greeting all, surprised everyone by speaking quietly as she stood next to a now seated Benton.

"Ben, when are you coming home? Your daughter has her graduation dance tonight and you promised to take her?"

"Olivia, I am busy. It's been a long day. Two concrete jobs. At this moment, I am interested in some peace and quiet."

"Well, what about Barbara?"

"You take her. I have to get up early tomorrow anyway. Please go away, Olivia."

Olivia did not move but then raised her voice, such was her frustration.

"You thorough bastard! So many broken promises."

Olivia lashed out with her open hand to smack Benton across the face. He brushed her arm aside without spilling his beer. Olivia picked up another bloke's half full beer and threw it in Benton's face.

Benton had had enough, dripping - he roughly escorted Olivia out of the bar and into her car. Then it was on for young and old as fists were flying everywhere as the car negoitiated exiting the car park, stopping and starting as the husband and wife traded blows. Unfortunately, it was far too often a scene. Poor Barbara, their daughter was late for her graduation.

Days later Benton was working when his phone rang. It was his 'girlfriend' -woman he visited on a regular but not frequent basis.

"Benny, when am I gunna see you?"

"I'm working girlfriend. I will ring you later Gracey. Keep the fires burning."

"I will wait then for the call, you big animal."

Grace Jenning was a sidelined single woman wanting a permanent arrangement with Benton but feared that she could not compete with the still beautiful Olivia, after fifteen years of marriage. Her looks hid a malevolent desire to control her husband Ben. A growing source of friction for Benton

The NSW Police deal with domestic violence daily despite National campaigns to reduce the threats to women and children in their homes. Olivia had told visiting Police her side of the violence and that she had nightmares;

"I wake constantly not knowing how any day is going to pan out."

Both Police Officers today noted Olivia's bright personality and attractive nature. In contrast, Olivia was fearful during the conversation. Olivia became friendly and welcoming but then depressive as she revealed many days ended badly with some sort of altercation and violent behaviour.

"I'm losing weight and suffering from depression. I'm locked in a cycle that some days prevents me from going to work."

The Police made notes then departed. They filed a routine report to a developing file.

The malevolent Grace Jenning was scheming to get Ben Hull to herself. She knew she could not compete with Olivia's looks, so she came up with a plan to send Olivia to hell with a gift of some facial cream via Benton. A gift for forgiveness, from a very sorry but recalcitrant husband. This facial cream, was a product with a topical poison in it. Olivia commenced to use it immediately to enhance her skin. The effect in a few days saw Olivia start to lose her hair in handfuls and an erupting rash developed on her face that would not heal and drove the vain woman, that Olivia was to complete distraction and in time away from the marriage finally.

Meanwhile Benton became disgusted with his now ugly wife and contemplated a divorce but he needed grounds. With his history of violence, he decided to maybe just leave Olivia. A clean break.

Olivia, irreversibly disfigured by the facial cream, screams with the pain each morning. She finally realises how toxic the cream must be and throws it away. Not thinking that her husband has poisoned her.

Olivia hit rock bottom and commited suicide cursing Benton with her dying breath. Her spirit becomes vengeful and tricks Benton into murdering his new live in lover, Gracey. The method includes Benton commencing to have nightmares and migraines. He is unable to work and sits at home with Grace regretting his actions which he knows led Olivia to take her own life.

Simon Dang gets involved at this point as the interviewing Police filed a report which asks more questions than it answers. Senior Police refer the file to Simon for an opinion. One reading gives Simon the 'horrors'.

He shakes with anger at the behaviour that wastes lives and wonder how to sort out a mess like this.

Simon gladly made some notes then put the file away. It was deplorable circumstance but he felt hopeless to affect change.

The phone rang next day with a Senator of the Australian Parliament on the line. Social Services Minister, Anne Rushton.

"Hi Simon, I am Anne Rushton."

"Yes, Minister I am aware of your current 'hot potato' portfolio. What can I do for you?"

"Simon, let me be frank, as I am aware of your status and work. We have spent a zillion in eight years on our Action Plan to reduce the scourge of domestic violence. The campaign has brought awareness

I am certain but we have barely scratched the surface. You may be aware of the Benton Hull case?"

"Yes, Minister. Please continue."

"It saddens me to have this behaviour still going on when our measures are dysfunctional and the scale of this domestic violence problem is inaccurate. I need your help?"

"Minister, you are on a hiding to nothing trying to track and control human behaviour-acceptable or not. Look at the behaviour on our roads for example. One thing I will say is this Benton Hull case ended with black magic. Whether you believe in such things or not is not for me to comment but I am horrified by what has transpired before the demise of this particular individual."

"Black magic Simon, this is unexpected! Can you elaborate?"

Simon went to great lengths to explain the occult.

"Simon, can you speculate with any certainty that the spirit of Benton Hull's wife, Olivia, haunted Benton Hull since she committed suicide. When Grace Jenning, Benton's girlfriend is implicated by Police as the source of the toxic facial cream and charged, Benton goes over the edge realising he has ruined many lives, including his daughter's. Declared insane, he is committed."

"Yes Minister. Olivia Hendersen's haunting spirit grows more and more intense in her influence. Finally Benton Hull goes insane. In Long Bay Goal awaiting trial for the murder (before the fact) of his deceased wife Olivia.

"Will you commit that to the file notes?"

"No problem. I am confident that this may be explanation."

"Simon, are the perpetrators of domestic violence mentally disturbed?"

"Certainly Minister."

Silence on the line.

"Thank you for your insightful discussion. Your reputation is well deserved and I hope to meet you one day."

Simon afterwards rang Bella to wish her a 'Happy Birthday' to counteract his depression. Bella responded as only a lover could.

Printed in the United States
By Bookmasters